HONORING
CHRISTMAS

HONORING CHRISTMAS

A Historical Romance by an Amish Author

LINDA BYLER

New York, New York

The characters and events in this book are the creation of the author,
and any resemblance to actual persons or events is coincidental.

HONORING CHRISTMAS

Library of Congress Cataloging-in-Publication Data is available on file.

Print ISBN: 978-1-68099-922-8
eBook ISBN: 978-1-68099-939-6

Cover by Godfredson Design

Printed in the United States of America

HONORING CHRISTMAS

Chapter 1

HENRY LIVED BESIDE THE JUNIATA RIVER IN THE year of our Lord 1823 in a moldy, rat-infested little bungalow that never seemed to be quite dry, or warm, or serene.

He was fourteen years old, finished with schooling, an apprenticed stable boy who served a master named Charles Rusk, the owner of a four-story hotel situated on the banks of the same river a few miles downstream.

A bridge made of stone brought pioneers across the river, the road leading to Ohio, Indiana, and the great unsettled West beyond.

He was one of thirteen children, all housed in the sagging old cabin by the river, another mouth to be fed by the thin, gaunt, overworked mother who had reconciled herself to life with an alcoholic husband. At one time, there had been hope, hope of redemption from the sordid life into which she had been coerced by the smiling charm of a handsome young man already swilling cheap brew hidden all over his father's farm. But as years went by, a child born almost every year, circumstances deteriorating into what she could only describe as desperate, she simply moved through her days going from one task to another without complaint.

Henry was fifth in line, a child always inclined to happiness, no matter how dire the situation was at the time. He was the one, the only one, resembling the husband in his youth, the thick wavy brown hair, the dancing brown eyes, and the dark complexion of the Italian in his ancestry. He was born on a summer morning when the dew sparkled on the bayberry bushes, the Muscovy ducks waddled through rain-kissed grass on their way to the river, and there was a sack of flour in the pantry, a burlap bag of oats, milk in the springhouse from the sad brown Guernsey cow with jutting hipbones and slatted ribs.

She looked into the perfect face of her fifth child, recognized the Italian, laid the tip of her forefingers gently on the dimple in his chin, and laughed out loud.

Her father. He so resembled her father. She counted him as a gift from God. He was named Henry.

Catherine, at that time, still created her own hope of her world being righted somehow, someday, after being swept off her sturdy brogues she wore in Ireland by the irresistible lure of the young man, the dark Italian named Gilbert Giovanni. She was ferried across the Atlantic on the wet *Bluebird*, creaking hull and unfurled sails, sailors brawling and swearing, a journey already taking her sunny disposition by storm.

She was so homesick it took a toll on her physically—she lost her girlish glow and the dancing blue of her eyes was never to be seen again.

They journeyed from Philadelphia to the wilds of northern Pennsylvania, and the house was built erratically by a husband fallen into bad company, having had acquired the thirst at a young age, although he hid it away quite effectively from the fairest young woman in Europe. Catherine Miller, the Irish lass with flaming red hair and eyes of emerald green, a laugh like the tinkling of tiny brass bells.

The years had not been kind after the courtship and marriage, however, with Gilbert Giovanni's restless eyes, his twitching hands and longing for greater opportunity in America. And so she surrendered to his will, felt it the one honorable thing to do, was tight-lipped, courageous even, as she tearfully said goodbye to her parents.

She would always remember the first time she found her husband lying on the doorstep, the odor leaking from his opened mouth, the shine of the spittle on his chin, a drunkard, inebriated, unable to lift himself off the stone steps leading to the front door. She forgave him, confronted with those anxious pleas, the light catching the waves of his thick brown hair as he sat with his head in his hands.

But by the time Henry was born, a light inside of her had been extinguished, replaced by a hardened callus, all that remained of her heart. As Henry grew from a winsome child to a budding young man, her road of life had been paved with heartache, nervous tension, disappointment as thick and cloying as the mold growing beneath the ivy on the walls of the house.

Henry found employment at the hotel, in the face of starvation, out of sheer, driving need. The drinking had worsened over the years, as the number of children had multiplied, so that their existence changed to desperation.

Charles Rusk was over six feet tall, a great bearded giant with arms and legs like tree trunks, with ownership of the grand four-story hotel under his belt, ambition his god, and a no-nonsense approach to every obstacle in his path.

So when the thin Giovanni boy stood before him with the hard light in his dark eyes, he saw a young man of fair spreadable consistency, hungry enough to do as he was told and accept a mere pittance as salary. He needed the help, figured his profits, and took him on.

It was a bitter day in March when Henry swung open the great oak stable doors, his ungloved hands red with the cold, shivering beneath his coat, the only thing covering his head the shock of thick wavy hair. He stopped inside, shook his reddened hands, cupped them to his mouth and blew. He stamped his feet, then peered into stalls, nodding his head, realizing what he imagined had happened.

The pioneers were starting this early.

Two new horses, no, three, four. Sturdy looking, with broad backs and heavy legs, muscular shoulders and haunches. He drew back on the cast iron latch, slid back the heavy gate, and stood, transfixed.

"Hey there, big fella," he whispered.

The horse turned his head, his large brown eyes like liquid coal. Henry extended a hand. The horse lipped his palm, soft and warm, and he laid the side of his cheek against the golden, noble head.

"What're doing in there, kid? Get outa there. C'mon, we have no time to waste."

The voice was like thunder, the eyes raining the hail of his disapproval, hurtful needles embedded in his ears.

"Get on outa there," Charles repeated, cuffing his ear with the side of his hammy fist. Tears rose to the surface; a painful blush rose to his windburned face, but he set his jaw and took the reprimand. He had no choice. The only thing between his family and cold and hunger was the eight or ten dollars he earned every other week. Sometimes twelve, if he would be fortunate enough to be thrown an extra dime, or quarters, from an appreciative traveler.

His stomach rolled and a moment of weakness overtook him. He'd run, then walked the miles of trail to the hotel, having done without breakfast. It would be another month before the cow freshened, so there was no milk, and the ground corn was low in the bag, the bread gone as well, his mother taken with the usual congestive cough of winter.

As he lifted the pitchfork off the wall, he thought perhaps he'd get lucky and the cook would allow him a crust of bread with lard. His mouth watered, thinking of the warm bread rising on the great wooden table running the length of the servants' kitchen.

"Put a move on there. S'wrong with you? Didn't you have no breakfast?"

Before he had a moment to answer, the oak door was flung open and a face like a skeleton appeared beneath a wide-brimmed hat.

"Look. I don't want no shoddy oats for my team. I'm paying a good price to be here for the night, so you better see they get fed well," he ground out in a consumptive growl, his small eyes set back in his hollow cheeks emanating no good will toward anyone, least of all the innkeepers he suspected of charging him far above what he deemed fair.

Charles Rusk grunted some noncommittal reply, and Henry slipped past the thin man in the broad hat and began the cleaning of stables. As he worked, the ache in his ear lessened, his hands lost their numbness, and he felt alive, ready to face whatever life threw in his direction, for today.

By midmorning, he was seriously lagging, his stomach hollow, his strength ebbing like the water under the bridge before him. Upending the wheelbarrow, he looked around for signs of spring, but could see no change except for a few breakups of the ice around the stone pillars supporting the bridge. He stopped to listen as a redbird called to another followed by the low tut-tuttering of the nuthatch, upside down on the side of a tree, his beak hammering on a crevice in the bark, searching for seeds he'd hidden there.

Why did God provide for the birds and not for his family? Why did he allow poverty, and alcoholic drinks, and a mother to bear thirteen of them, without hope?

The four oldest had all left, married very young to get away from the squalor, the sadness and hopelessness of the hollow eyes of their mother. The older siblings leaving put a crushing burden on Henry. It became his responsibility to provide a bit of normalcy for his seven siblings, shielding them from the worst of his father's homecomings, his mother's lack of . . . well, anything, really, only doing what was expected of her, barely noticing anything that occurred around her.

He shivered, closed the door, was thoroughly tired of winter. He decided to approach the cook, laid down his fork, peered right, then left, and finding the coast clear, made a feverish dash for the house.

Built into the side of a steep hill, it never failed to amaze him, the sheer size and immense strength of the sturdy brown rock used to build it. A massive front porch faced the river below, and the walls rose up three more stories, the wooden shutters accenting the beauty of this architecture.

He ran up the side steps and broke into the kitchen, praying he'd find a bit of compassion at this early hour.

A surly maid was punching bread dough, her brow furrowed in concentration, her large white apron slipping down the sides of her shoulders as she pounded. The cook was washing dishes in a great blue agate pan, soap suds up to her elbows, leaving stacks of white stoneware plates coupled with cups and glasses, silverware strewn like straw.

"Morning, Bertha," he ventured softly.

She turned to assess her visitor, never missing a step in her repetitious motion, scrubbing a pot in a circular motion.

"Whatcha up to, Henry?" she thundered.

"I was hoping you could spare a little something, I'm hollow inside."

"Not my fault. Why didn't ya eat breakfast? You get up too late."

He smiled ruefully, shook his head. He could never tell her of his situation, could never tell her about the drink, the tab at Closter's Store in Bloody Run, the hunger and fatigue, the wet and the cold when the mist froze on itself, the tiny flame on the hearth doing nothing to chase the chill on those mornings when his mother huddled with her children beneath filthy woolen blankets.

"Tell you what," the maid said quietly. "You carry the wood up to the third floor, clean the hearth, you can have the rest of the mush. A couple pieces o' flitch fell on the floor. You could have it."

"Shirley, now you ain't the boss, I am. If I say you take that wood up, you do it."

"Well, I would, but my stomach's paining me right bad." The cook lifted her hands from the dishwater, dried them on a dishtowel, clucked to herself, and headed for the back of the enormous cookstove, a recent acquisition, and one Charles Rusk crowed about to all his peers.

She lifted the lid, peered inside, then added a few sticks of wood through the opening of the range top. "You may as well come git it," she said, unenthused.

Henry was gleeful, filled with victory. Imagine mush and flitch. He lifted the pot lid, upended it, and scraped out the cornmeal mixed with water and salt, a warm, grainy cooked mush with the smell of roasted corn.

"Sugar?" he asked, putting on his most charming smile.

"You know better."

Scowling, she pushed a brown molasses jug in his direction, which he knew she would do, considered himself fortunate to have it. And milk, cold and creamy, creating a lovely swirl as he stirred it in. Then he sat with the bowl and spoon, ravenously lifting it again and again.

"Yer flitch," the maid said, pushing the pork bacon in his direction.

"Thank you." He bent his head, tore off a piece, and chewed, the grease and salt infusing his tongue.

"How's your mam and the little ones?" the cook asked. He nodded. "Good."

Bertha placed her swollen fingers on rounded hips and eyed him dubiously. She opened her mouth and closed it again.

Then she plunged right in.

"Henry, I've no idea why you don't talk about it. Abe Hunsecker done told me a while back about yer dat bein' a real drunk, how he goes from one bit o' work to the next, the whisky eatin' out his liver, his wife and kids starving like a pack of coyotes in the winter. They say he's over at Penny Shauf's place half the time."

She sucked her teeth, turned to look at him, her gaze piercing. The maid, Shirley, was motionless now, her mouth gaping in disbelief.

Henry continued eating, unhurried, silent. Shirley gave Bertha an uneasy look. When he finished, he rose to his feet, wiped his mouth with the back of his hand, and thanked them again.

Then he said, "I guess I can't always hide everything away. People will find things out, I suppose."

"Yes. Henry, they do. And I'm sorry."

"It's alright."

And with that, he was gone, leaving Bertha to shake her head as her cheeks flamed with frustration. Many a young lad had been buried by the sins of the fathers, the curse of alcohol snaking out to grasp their young legs and throw them unwittingly, leave them to grovel on the ground, desperately trying to get away, to free themselves from the generational sin.

"Now there's a fine lad goin' to waste, if he takes after that lyin' father, thievin' across the town, without a conscience, that wife a' his an empty soul."

"I heard he's been with that Penny Shauf. She used to be the schoolteacher."

"Well, she ain't now," Bertha said shortly, her eyes popping with anger. "Shirley, I want you to scrape together whatever is left over, even the potato peels. Keep some back before you slop the hogs."

Chapter 2

HENRY CARRIED A SLING OF WOOD ON HIS BACK up one story, then two, and finally the third, his eyes taking in the finery of embellished wallpaper, heavy ornate trim work with intricate wood grain, a fireplace crackling with a warm fire in every room, sunshine through heavy panes of glass. Warm, with the most wonderful scent of woodsmoke, cooking, and soap. Dry, the whole house was so blessedly dry and warm.

He found the designated room, the fire burned to a heap of gray ashes, took up the cast iron poker, and stirred before placing the wood directly on it. He cast a quick look around the bedroom, the high four-poster bed with the elaborate cover, too many pillows to count, a wooden chest along the foot. A brown dresser with porcelain knobs, a mirror attached to an intricate frame, rugs, chairs, a trunk opened in the corner.

He caught sight of his face in the mirror, the heavy shock of wavy brown hair, the thin face with eyes too large for it.

At fourteen, he was still a boy, though he had responsibilities most men would find daunting, and after Bertha's speech, he felt the alarming spread of a slow burr of anger, the spark of outrage and indignation having grown to something else.

Something he knew would change things.

He turned away as he heard footfalls, hushed on the carpeted hallway. He moved quickly, away from the mirror, as if he had done something wrong. As he went through the door, he met an older woman, tall, haughty, her hair done up a in a high, powdered style, her sweeping skirts like a red blossom of gathers and flounces.

"Well, young man. What were you doing in my room?" she inquired, her beady blue eyes wide.

"Stoking the fire, ma'am."

He bowed, one arm to his waist, the other behind his back, before straightening, almost as tall as she, his gaze clear and unblemished.

"I ask you not to return. I've taken a chill and wish to retire for a lengthy nap."

"Certainly, ma'am."

"See that you stay away."

He nodded, turned away, thought this would always be his lot in life, bowing, obeying, surrendering to those in a higher position, paid the minimum of available wages, always hungry, cold in winter. He was forced into this, a provider for the family, earning enough to keep them alive, enough to keep them all from freezing.

There was no choice. He thought of his mother, her thin frame lost in the dresses she wore, faded and mended, moth-eaten, and not clean, her greasy hair falling into her pale face, her teeth rotted or missing. Had she once been young and beautiful, with a laugh and eyes that sparkled?

A fresh rage coursed through him, one both frightening and exhilarating. Penny Shauf, huh? So that was the reason he often stayed away at night. His mother need not know, however, need not have this awful truth on top of her sad existence.

"Henry!"

He stopped. Mrs. Rusk stood below him as he came down the stairs, florid in her purple finery, her face red with exertion.

"I need you to help me move the sofa in the drawing room. I lost my thimble, and I believe it rolled underneath."

"Yes, ma'am."

He scraped and bowed, then followed her down the short hallway to a door on the left. Flowered rugs covered the wide oak planks of the floor and warm fire leaped and danced from freshly laid logs. There was a kaleidoscope of furniture, plants, brocade curtains, and sunlight, everything as warm and dry as it had been upstairs.

"Here. Under this sofa."

She pointed a forefinger, round and fat as a sausage, covered with two or three silver rings. A round wooden hoop with unfinished embroidery work was flung on the cushions.

Dutifully, Henry got down on his knees, lowered his face to peer below the sofa, but found nothing. Straightening, he grasped the arm, lifted, and moved it away a few feet, which revealed the small object immediately. He bent to pick it up, handed it over, and set the couch in the usual position.

"You're dismissed, Henry."

He'd learned not to expect a thank you. Just doing his duty.

* * *

He walked home in the bitter March wind, following the line of trees along the Juniata River. The ice was thick, had covered most of it all winter, but he could see where the spring sunshine was corroding it along the edges. Dark branches of oak were stretched across the sky, patchy white sycamore closer to the water.

He rounded a slight bend and came upon the small brown hovel built into the steep hillside covered in trees, a thin line of smoke coming from the chimney, the wooden shakes on the roof covered in moss, some of them cracked or broken.

Brown weeds hung against the gray logs, bits of wood chips mixed with dirty snow leading up to the front door. They'd never had a porch, his father insisting he'd never seen the need of one. Folks could sit in their houses.

He smelled failure, hopelessness, a sense of doom. A heightened awareness of this grasped him in slimy tentacles, squeezed out any hopeful plan or a design for a better way of life. When he lifted the latch, he was caught in a panic, the need to get away from this, to find a life away from this sadness. He took a breath, willing himself to accept the unavoidable.

His father was at home, sitting silently at the kitchen table, leaning against the back of a chair, one thin arm draped across the table, the other dangling by his side. He wore a week's worth of stubble on his gaunt face, his beard yellowed and matted, his eyes swollen, rheumy, his nose already purpled and mottled with blue veins.

His mother stood at the fireplace, her back turned as she stirred something in the blackened kettle, her narrow waist rising above the limp fall of gathers.

She turned, her pale face taut with tension. She caught his eye, nodded tersely.

"Here." He thrust the parcel tied with twine at her.

"What is it?"

"From the hotel. The cook sent it."

Potato bits, bits of onion, a purple beet, stale crusts of bread. But her eyes shone, as much as was possible. Quietly, she separated the bits of food and squirreled them away in the near empty pantry.

The house was dark, the acrid smell of mold and mildew his first sensation. But today there was another smell, another sharper odor, like vinegar.

"Henry." His father motioned for him to come closer.

He looked in the general direction of his father, said nothing.

"Henry." He spoke gruffly but quietly, as if sharing a secret. "I want you to know first, before I tell your mother." He cleared his throat, slid his eyes in her direction. The crackle of the fire concealed his voice, he thought.

"You're a man now. I want you to know that. You can take care of Mam and the rest of you. I'm leaving and I'm not coming back. It's your mother's fault."

His eyes moved again toward his long-suffering wife, who was still, as still as stone, her eyes flat, hooded, showing nothing.

"She doesn't love me anymore, or so it seems. She won't be a wife to me, so I found another who does love me. Your mother hasn't always been nice to me since we came to America, so it drove me to drink. She knows this, and has come to accept it."

Shock went through Henry's body like waves, impeding his vision, the ability to think, obscuring common sense, followed by the roaring of red-hot rage in his ears. How dare he blame his poor mother? How dare he leave them? All the anger he'd kept subdued for so long came flying to the surface. In one leap he was at the kitchen table, his father's filthy stiffened shirtfront in his fist, clawing, lifting, his other hand drawing back for the first blow.

His father was still bigger than he was, though, and he caught his arm easily, wrestled him down, sat on the slight form, and hit his head, his neck, and shoulders, grunting, saliva flying from his open mouth.

Henry fought, twisted his body to protect himself with his arms, but was easily overpowered. Spent and broken, he lay quietly, willing the blows to stop.

The small children heard the commotion and came in where they huddled in the corner and covered their eyes or ears, their thin, pale faces conveying a peculiar mixture of acceptance and fear.

Suddenly there was a high keening cry, his mother in white-faced fury, the cast iron poker held aloft. She brought it down on her husband's back, eliciting a roar of pain and outrage. He scrambled to his feet, red-faced and bloated, hurling accusations, grabbing the poker.

She held on, held him at bay with her terrible gaze. "You will leave, yes, and I wish you Godspeed. Don't ever darken this doorway again, ever."

He backed away from her, flung out an arm as if to speak, took one wild-eyed look at his son still lying on the floor, a sweep of his gaze to the children wide-eyed in the corner. He choked. Spittle ran down his chin.

"I . . . I don't want to do this, God knows."

"You do. Go."

And he went, stumbling backward before retracing his steps, coming forward, opening his mouth, but no sound came from it. In the end, he merely let himself out the door and closed it behind him, softly.

Silence was broken by the smallest one, a girl named Judith, who wailed softly and walked over to her mother to hide in her skirts. Henry struggled to his feet while the children straggled to the table, one by one, searching first their mother's face, then Henry's.

"There isn't much more to say. We'll have our supper." Her voice shook only a little.

A thin porridge, glasses of water, but it filled their growling stomachs.

During the night, the wind come up, howling around the house, loose shakes straining as branches whipped across the roof. It woke Henry, who wasn't quite sure if it was the wind or the high keening of his mother's grief that he heard.

* * *

News traveled fast in the small community of Bloody Run. Mr. Closter, of Closter's General Store, shook his head and marked Catherine Giovanni's tab with a red X. Paid in full, he proudly told his wife. The ladies at sewing circle gathered all their leftover pieces of fabric and laid them aside, held a meeting at Adelphia Stone's house, complete with tea and hot cross buns, and came up with a plan to approach Catherine and find out what clothing they could sew for her.

At the hotel, Henry was greeted with vague curiosity, which turned to pointed questions from the cook. Henry was spreading horse manure on the garden behind the kitchen, when the door was flung open and Bertha positioned herself at the edge, her arms wrapped around her waist in the chilly wind.

"What gives with yer face? All them blue bruises, all them scratches? Ye got inna fight?"

Henry kept on forking manure. "No."

"Heard yer dat left."

"Yes."

"Why so?"

"Oh well, you know. It's the drink."

"Yeah, I know. Took down many a good man. What's yer mam to do?"

"We've done without him before."

"Well, Henry, let it be known. I'm calling on Charles Rusk, so I am. If you're the breadwinner, I'll see to it you can win some bread, too."

Henry's head was throbbing in pain, the space behind his eyes exploding with a white light that lit up frequently, his lips swollen and cracked. Still, Charles Rusk was repeatedly telling him to get a move on, time was wasting away. The fact that he had no choice but to surrender spurred him on. Two new wagon-loads arrived late in the afternoon, the horses of the first lathered with white foam, stretching their necks as they eased the heavy wagon across the Juniata. The occupants of the wagon seat looked weary with lack of sleep and the tedious hours on the road, the rhythmic plodding of horses, the creak of the wagon wheels, the flap of heavy canvas in the March wind.

But they greeted Henry warmly, the gladness to be able to enjoy a good bed and a meal before embarking on the grueling leg of their westward journey shining from their eyes.

"How do ya do, son?" yelled the first passenger, his wife sitting beside him, clutching a toddler, his eyes conveying a message that was anyone's guess.

"Hello," Henry answered, ashamed of his bruises, aware of the scrutiny, the withheld questions hinging on good manners.

"You take care o' the horses. I'll see to my wife."

Nodding, Henry didn't smile, his lips cracking and bleeding if he tried.

He didn't care what anyone thought of him, didn't know them at all, and they certainly didn't know who he was either.

He took care of the horses, rubbed them down with pieces of burlap, watered them and gave them a portion of oats and hay. Charles was always present, so talk turned to him and Henry was forgotten, which suited him fine.

The second wagon was bigger, with a large black-bearded man wearing a broad-brimmed hat, his eyes as yellow and as piercing as the gaze of an eagle. He was loud, effusive in his greeting, his wife big-boned and as tall as he, but mercifully quiet, her features downcast, her face as pale as the broken ice on the river.

A face appeared behind her, then another. Two sets of eyes lit on his face, alive with curiosity, but the mother told them to get down, their father would open the back when he thought necessary. Henry heard some distant wails about a pig in a poke and smiled in spite of himself, then winced as his lower lip tore open again.

He repeated the process, providing feed, water, and comfort for the horses, swept every wisp of hay and scattered oats, then found it was time to call it a day. He gathered up his threadbare coat and went to the side door of the kitchen.

Shirley handed him a reed basket, which he hooked over one arm, thanked her politely, and turned to go.

As he walked down the curing drive to the bridge, crossed over and turned right, he was brought sharply back to reality. He felt exhausted thinking of home, his grieving mother and bewildered siblings.

So much depended on him. Mouths to feed, a house to keep up, firewood and no one to help.

Could it be, however, that it might prove to be easier, knowing he could do what needed to be done without fear of his father?

With a newfound sense of purpose, he lengthened his stride, lifted his shoulders, and winced at the pain.

Chapter 3

SPRING CAME VERY SOFTLY, STEALING HEARTS like a band of handsome suitors, turning hillsides green, then brilliant with dandelions. In the forest, ferns unfurled, streams ran full, and the heady scent of purple lilac invaded even the most stoic hearts, turning thoughts to younger years, when bones didn't creak and ache with arthritis, when graying hair was thick and sprang away with the fullness of curls.

Henry longed for a barn, a few sheep, a pig to fatten, a study board fence, but knew these things were not within his reach. So he contented himself by working around the house in his spare hours, with the help of his brother David and tomboy sister Annabelle—Belle for short.

They pulled off the cloying ivy, used the lye soap and stiff brushes, cleaned away the mold and residue of the creeping plant. He repaired broken shakes on the roof, daubed mud in the chinks between logs.

They pulled weeds and scythed the lawn, dug a garden with borrowed hand shovels.

With food leftover from the hotel and Mr. Closter saving them bags of potatoes, flour, and molasses, the children regained their health and became rosy-cheeked and vibrant with life.

Their mother, however, remained in a state of sadness. She sat with vacant eyes and a dejected slump of her thin shoulders, staring off through rooms as if she could see beyond the log walls. She rarely spoke, except to snap at the toddler hiding in her skirts, crying, wiping his nose that seemed to run continuously.

There were no windows along the back of the house, so Henry spent days cutting in two windows, clearing brush and weeds, relishing the fresh air flowing through. It should help with the mold, he reasoned.

His shoulders widened, his arms rounded as a stubble of growth appeared on his upper lip and along his jaw.

* * *

The house by the river was still small, but it had been transformed into a pleasant little cottage, the windows cleaned, the grass scythed, a large garden growing in the new clearing. Henry was sixteen and his sister Belle, just a year younger, had grown into a slim young girl who took a bright-eyed interest in working alongside Henry. Together, they'd made a difference.

The midsummer sun was sliding below the line of trees across the river, creating a golden light on the rippling waters of the Juniata. Dragonflies hovered and a mild hum of flies and mosquitoes mingled with the tinkling of low water over rock. In the background, there was noise of children at play, shrieks and cries as they ran between trees, dodging each other like young colts.

"Henry, what do you think about Mother?" Belle began, turning to pluck a blade of grass and blow on the edge, trying to produce a harsh whistle, but could only create an impotent puff of air.

He turned to look at her, his long brown hair thick and wavy, a lock falling over his forehead.

"What about her?"

"She doesn't seem right. Says less and less. I have to keep after her to stay clean, to care about the children. I'm thinking of asking at the hotel for work. Perhaps she'll get herself going if I am no longer here."

"You can't do that."

"I could. What scares me most is the vacant look in her eyes, like she's not here at all, but someplace we can't follow. She never cries or laughs, and rarely talks."

"I know."

"We need clothes, shoes, winter coats."

"I'll ask Charles for more pay. I've taken on working on wagons, oiling, repairing. Sometimes they'll allow me an extra dime. Last week I got a quarter."

"The Baptist Church in Bloody Run . . ."

"No."

Belle looked over, her blue eyes boring into his.

"Why?"

"I won't go there. They're pompous, self-righteous folks who think they know everything. We're nothing and you know it."

"But they . . ."

"No."

"Why?"

"Because I don't believe in a God who serves favors to certain people and forgets about others."

"You mean us?"

"Well yes. Of course."

Belle considered this, then nodded her head.

Henry looked out across the slow-moving water, his brown eyes squinting in the fading light.

"We're getting by, Belle. And we're doing it on our own. We don't owe anyone a dime. I'm going to approach Charles for more money, for sure, and if he agrees to a raise, we'll see about clothes."

"But Henry, it's the winter coats. It's shoes. You'll never make enough to provide those things. The last coats Father got from the Ladies' Auxiliary in Bedford. There are nine of us, and I can do with a shawl, but not the little ones who walk to school with barely enough to eat and no meat on their bones to keep them warm."

They both sat on the riverbank, Belle's knees pulled up beneath her gathered skirt, Henry's long legs stretched out, saying nothing, turning over and over the facts of the turn their life had taken.

Their father had been sighted from time to time on a seat atop a lumbering wagon, with Penny Shauf at his side. Henry had met his eyes, once, but his father had quickly turned away, refusing to acknowledge him.

Henry stood his ground, watched the mud-splattered buckboard pass, the rage welling up afterward as he bent and picked up a stone, lifted his arm, and hurled it after the retreating couple.

His mother never left the few acres, the house by the river. Women from the church had ceased all attempts at friendship, but worried about the vacant stare from beneath the lined forehead topped by prematurely gray hair, a woman appearing far older than she was. Their requests that she join them for Sunday service were always met with the same reply—a silent, if strong, refusal by a shaking of her head from side to side.

They got by with regular contributions from the hotel kitchen, the only place Henry ever filled his stomach, ever felt the goodness of having enough.

After the few attempts at joking about getting out of bed too late, Bertha realized the young man's deprivation, the searing, bone-chilling hunger in his eyes, and fed him without hesitation. No one knew if a few slices of bread, ground oats, or an extra egg went missing.

The two women in the kitchen were a conduit for news of his father, of the town's life, the gossip and goings on about Bloody Run. There was another hotel being built in the center of town, but this one right here was the one for the good country folk, the farmers from southern Pennsylvania and Maryland who had a hankering for the lure of the West.

They came in sturdy wagons, the canvas cover rising up over the metal hoops secured to the sides, the front seat high and sturdy, made of thick slabs of oak, polished to a good serviceable shine. The men, for the most part, were simple, open-faced farmers, hearty and with a good disposition, their wives' skin toasted brown, sunbonnets slung over their shoulders in disregard for all they'd been taught. They were on their own now, going west. They were pioneers, freed from the restrictions of their Catholic rules. Or

Protestant, some of them Baptist or Lutheran, but all of them escaping the confines of the organized religion they'd been raised under.

And there were the brawlers, the drunken men without women and children, a group who had heard of panned gold nuggets, their eyes alight with greed, impatient, uncouth.

Henry dreaded these arrivals, with their stink and crude jokes, sticking elbows into his ribs with lewd innuendos, their mouths open wide, showing teeth like rows of yellowed corn as they laughed uproariously. At first he stayed out of their way, but as a year went by, his resentment boiled over into anger, which fortified his resolve and gave him courage.

The morning was already hot, the sun rising above the mountain in a pulsing orange ball of heat, the air thick with humidity and darting insects. Henry paused in his work to roll up his sleeves, lift an arm to wipe the sweat off his forehead, run a hand through his thick hair.

He heard them when they were a long way off, already drinking midmorning, hollering and singing as they traveled along the base of the bridge.

He was ready to replace the great heavy wheel on Mr. Jakes's wagon, a powerful farmer who'd been staying for most of a week, allowing his wife and children a rest, a few days in town, carefully purchasing the things they might need.

He pressed his lips in firm resolve, recognizing the need to be a man. To hide, or wish he could, was no longer an option.

So he bent to his task, his hair hiding his face as the untidy wagon with the sweating horses ground its way across the bridge, down the gravelly incline, and into the stable yard.

Henry stayed at his work, bent over the axle of the wagon, till a rough voice called out, "Hey. Hey you, there."

He stood up slowly, his eyes flattened in the strong sunlight. "Good morning," he said levelly.

"Well, if it ain't a pretty boy."

He was sized up from head to toe, in a long hard gaze from two small eyes, heavy eyebrows raised in a mocking expression.

"How much to feed these critters, give us some breakfast?"

"I'll get the boss."

"Fair enough."

He found Charles beneath the shed roof, repairing a bridle. Even from a distance, he could tell things were not going well, the way he was swearing and jerking on the leather.

"A couple of men. How much to feed the animals?"

"You know as much as I do about the stable, kid. You don't have to bother me about these things. Tell 'em."

He strode back, his feet hitting the ground with new purpose, told the men a dollar for both horses.

He was assessed with a mean look from the driver, the passenger beside him puffing on a stubby cigar, his long hair in great strands parted by protruding red ears, smashed down by the filthy old hat, the brim waving upward in front, a silent salutation.

"S'too much," he bellowed, his chin wet with drool, his dark beard shiny with it.

"That's what it is," Henry answered, his eyes unwavering.

"Yer crazy."

Henry shrugged, turned away, and began his task on the wheel.

"Aright. Git over here, young man. Git over here and unhitch, take care of 'em."

Henry straightened, walked over, and caught the reins thrown from the sweat. He looked the horses over, saw the small size, the exhaustion, the swelling ankle on the horse hitched to the right side. Both had sunken eyes, the mouths dry, the bit too secure on a bridle buckled too short. They'd never make it, not out of Pennsylvania, he bet.

"Your horses have water today?" he asked, busying himself undoing traces, tying up the driving reins.

"Nope. Didn't have time."

"You know you can't do that," Henry said, in a voice stronger than he'd planned.

Instantly, he felt the man beside him, the stench of leather, unwashed clothes and body, the fermented scent of whatever they were drinking. A powerful, hammy fist lifted the waistband of his trousers and jerked him upward, almost lifting him off his feet.

"Yer too big fer yer britches, you upstarts. Who do ye think ye are? The Pope?"

A hot anger sizzled through him, but he knew his family's existence hung in the balance, so he put both hands on his thighs and tugged his trousers back into place, reached back to tuck his shirt in.

"Just saying. You'll get more miles out of them if you keep them watered."

Both men stood, eyeing him with distaste, their faces covered in facial hair, cheeks like rotten tomatoes. Before further exchange, there was a rumpus in the back of the wagon, a pile of blankets moved, and the dirtiest hair and face Henry had ever seen was thrust upward. Henry saw hands gripping the back of the seat, the dark face filled with frightened brown eyes at sight of him. She disappeared behind the seat again.

"Come on, Lila. Git out. Git yersel' down if yer hungry."

Wild-eyed, her hair stiff with filth, her dress covered in grease and dirt, she leaped over the side and hit the ground, like a cat, then stood glaring at him, as if to dare him to come closer. Henry looked back, then to the two men, imagining the worst.

"She ain't what you think," the man in the upturned hat chortled. "She's mine. My daughter."

Did he imagine, or was there the slightest shake of her head? Her eyes fell away when he tried holding her gaze.

Was she really his daughter?

He showed them the way to the hotel dining room, wondering at the stench, how Bertha would react, but said nothing. Aa they moved off, he saw the girl was fairly tall, thin, but had a strong loping walk. Was she an Indian?

His curiosity kept him standing with the horses until they moved up the wide steps and into the hotel. Only then did he turn, drawing on the reins, leading the thirsty horses to a long cast-iron trough filled with fresh water.

"Poor buggers," he said aloud, bending to run a hand across the swollen ankle, up the leg to the swollen knee above it. He whistled low, raised his eyebrows.

The team of horses drank and drank, the sound of the good water going down their throats like a regular heartbeat, a sound he loved to hear. These horses weren't bad, they were simply too small for the clumsy wagon, too small for the projected distance.

He led them to a box stall, tied them to feed troughs, and forked their hay, then scattered oats from a scoop. His stomach rumbled and he headed for Bertha's kitchen. The interior was dark and he needed time to adjust his eyesight to the long wooden table spread with dishes, rising bread dough, a steaming kettle on the cookstove, and the heavenly aroma of sizzling sausages.

The swinging doors of the dining room swung open and a red-faced Shirley thumped through, her eyes spitting outrage.

"I'm not going back out there," she hissed.

Bertha looked up, clearly exasperated. "I don't have time."

"Well, you're going. I'm not."

Sighing, Bertha put down the wooden spoon.

"What happened?"

"He touched me, that's what happened. Smells worse than dead possum left in the sun, and he touched me here."

"Let me deal with him," Henry offered.

Bertha hesitated, knowing he smelled of horses. She nodded her head, figuring this these type of men probably smelled worse.

When the tray of eggs and porridge was prepared, he took up the tray and swung through the heavy doors.

The dining room was fair-sized, with tables spread across oak floors, the walls papered with a design of greenery in long flowing wisps. Heavy drapes hung in matching colors beside a massive stone fireplace, with gas lights hung from the heavy ceiling beams.

He found them and strode purposefully across the room, stopping to unload the large tray. They watched in silence, asked for bread and more butter, before falling on their eggs like starving wolves.

Henry watched the girl from the corner of his eyes, saw her receive a dish of thick oatmeal and open her mouth to ask for something before closing it again. He placed a jug of molasses and a pitcher of milk at her elbow.

The men hadn't bothered removing their hats, so nothing was visible as they ate, the only sound a snuffling and loud, open-mouthed chewing.

One of them stopped, looked up with beady eyes. "Whatcha waitin' on? Git on wi' it."

Back in the kitchen, he grimaced, shook his head. "Must have been a month since any of them touched water, or washed clothes."

Bertha waved in disgust, but Shirley was still upset. She sat in a corner without speaking.

Returning with the bread and butter, he placed it at the girl's elbow, watched as she immediately grabbed a slice, but was stopped by a large grubby hand on her arm.

"Don't need that butter. We can't have you getting fat. Too much for the horses."

They threw back their heads and roared, drawing irate glances from across the room.

The laughter was long enough for the girl to lift her eyes, to see him for a few seconds, to shake her head back and forth with the slightest movement.

He blinked, raised his eyebrows, but lowered them immediately when the laughing was cut off abruptly.

"What you doin', standing there gawking at our Lila? Git away from us. Git."

He could hardly tear himself away, feeling like she
was trying to give him a secret message.

He moved off reluctantly and slowly pushed
through the swinging doors to find a plate of sausages
and bread and a drink of fresh milk, with Bertha sitting down with a cup of tea, which meant there was
news.

Chapter 4

HE RETURNED TO THE STABLE, CHUCKLING about Bertha's description of the ladies' sewing circle—Lady Rusk's inane demands for ice and lemons as soon as the temperature soared, the stuffiness of her darkened rooms with the shutters closed in the afternoon.

Bertha barked at Shirley to stop sitting there pitying herself, it wasn't the first time that had happened, and sure as God's green earth, it wouldn't be the last.

It seemed to him as if Bertha's kitchen was like a sanctuary, a safe place where he worshipped a sort of rough, earthy kindness. He was grateful, in a misunderstood sort of way, without even realizing it.

Later, as he worked, the sun rose higher and hotter, beating down on his back, soaking the rough homespun fabric.

He'd forgotten about the two men and was finishing the wheel with Charles Rusk's help when he heard the loud quarreling from the heavy cover of trees below the barn.

Charles straightened, watched as the two men sparred, carrying a corked bottle, engaged in loud conversation.

"I ain't doin' it," the one shouted. The other laid a hand on his arm, earnestly imploring, in garbled language, but with a hard shake, the hand fell away, the owner of it almost losing his balance.

"She'll sleep all afternoon," Henry heard clearly.

"I'm not goin' into Bloody Run."

"Hello, fellows," Charles greeted them.

Two pairs of drunken eyes peered up at him, the pupils swimming in every direction.

"Who're you?"

"I own the hotel. Charles Rusk. Pleased to make your acquaintance."

He stuck out a hand, sniffed, and instantly retracted it. He was sized up with bleary eyes, half-hearted attempts at staying upright, till the one remembered his manners and garbled, "Ezra Moon. At your service," followed by hysterical giggling from his companion.

"That ain't his name."

Charles frowned, then the color suffused his face.

"Look, you better put that bottle down. You're in no shape to be around my establishment. Get down to your wagon and sleep it off."

"Nope. No way. My daughter's down there sleeping. You keep an eye on her till we get back? We're goin' into town."

Instantly, the argument broke out again, fast and furious, till Charles parted them and pointed a finger toward Bloody Run. He watched as they swung off, determined to show they certainly were not inebriated, and promptly walked into a tree, righted themselves, and lurched off.

Charles shook his head.

Henry said nothing, his memory serving up many scenes of his childhood. The scent of fermentation, the sour breath and weaving walk, the set of his mother's mouth as she tried to give in to yet another day ending in despair, the way her shoulders stayed tense as he looked after the children, tried to protect them from the worst of it.

He hated alcohol. Any form of drink that would addle a brain, causing pain and heartache, a life scrambled by its effects.

"What did he say about a girl?" Charles asked, lifting the wagon tongue to push it out of the way.

"His daughter." Henry shoved his chin in the direction of the wagon.

"You think she is?"

Charles shifted the toothpick in his mouth, reached into his pocket for his handkerchief, and mopped his streaming brow.

Henry shrugged.

"Look, it's too hot to do much this afternoon. I'm going to keep my wife company a while. Why don't you try to talk to the girl. See what she says."

"You sure?"

"Yeah, I am. Just keep watch for anyone coming across the bridge."

Henry nodded, looking up to find a broad smile on Charles's face. "You know, Henry, you're my best man. I couldn't do without you. We'll have to see about things at the turn of the year."

Whatever that's supposed to mean, Henry thought as he walked away. He'd been cuffed and slapped around too many times to count, belittled for his clumsiness, raked across the coals with harsh words, but he'd hung on like a bulldog. Hung on to rake in the few coins that lay between his family and begging on the streets.

He approached the beat-up wagon, noticed the loose spokes, the rotting wagon bed, and knew coupled with the drink, they'd never make it. They'd travel a while, from tavern to tavern, until the money ran out, and they'd stay somewhere in Ohio, or Indiana if the horses held out.

He saw her, then, on a mound of woolen blankets. Her stiff hair was spread like a tumbleweed, coarse and filthy, her blackened face without prettiness. A wild child, really. Was she a daughter? If so, where was the mother?

He lifted a hand to swat at a yellow jacket, bumped a corner of the wagon, which was met with instant hysterics. She shot up, threw herself against a corner, her hands clawing, raking at the air, diabolical screams erupting in short hard jerks.

"No, no, don't," Henry begged, reaching out to stop her, which only increased the furious resistance, the wild desperation to be left alone.

Slowly realization dawned, and she slowed, but shrank into a corner of the wagon, her knees to her chin, her arms wrapped around them, her eyes wide with horror.

"I'm not going to hurt you," Henry said softly.

There was no answer, only the lifting of her top lip, like a catamount's snarl.

"Would you like to come with me to Bertha's kitchen?"

She shook her head violently, banging it against the seat, over and over, the sobbing starting up again.

Henry looked over his shoulder at the hotel, the brown stones glowing in the sun. Should he get Charles?

He waited, unsure. The sobbing slowed, then quieted. She rose to her knees, hung her head over the side, pressed on one nostril and blew the residue from her nose.

"I'm Henry. Henry Giovanni. Are you Lila?" he asked gently.

She nodded, looking at him through the mass of filthy hair fallen over her face.

"Your father and his traveling companion went into town. Would you like to meet Bertha and Shirley? Maybe they'll let you take a bath, wash your hair."

She spoke in a hoarse, unused voice, in a dialect unfamiliar to him.

He shook his head, lifted the palms of his hands. She switched to broken English.

"When . . . will. Be back?"

"They're drunk. They went to find a tavern, won't be back for a while."

"I must stay."

"You don't have to."

She caught her lower lip between her teeth, then reached up to push her hair out of her face. He noticed the high rounded cheekbones, the large brown eyes, and wondered.

"They come back?" she whispered hoarsely.

"No, not now."

She heaved herself over the side in the same lithe movement before standing beside him, surprisingly tall.

She was filthy, the smell of her overpowering, but he stayed, then led the way to the kitchen.

Lila was reluctant, hanging back at the door, refusing to acknowledge either Bertha or Shirley. She almost went in, then made a break for the door. Henry caught her wrist, begged her to stay. She refused a bath, but accepted a bar of soap, a towel, and clean clothes of Shirley's, then walked off to the river, alone.

An hour later, Henry went to find her, afraid she had made the senseless decision to run away. He moved quietly, up and down the riverbank, calling her name.

The air was very hot and still, the river smelling brackish as it often did in summer. He waited. He was used to listening for sounds others missed, hunting and trapping, so he was patient.

Finally, he heard it, a low, plaintive song. He moved toward it, over bare rock and soft ferns.

She sat beneath a towering willow, hidden by waving fronds, dressed in the green flowered dress of Shirley's, combing her long dark hair with her fingers. She was singing a sad song, her low voice tremulous with the words tumbling as slowly as an almost dry river in summer.

She was breathtakingly lovely.

The thought came to him unbidden, stole into his consciousness and literally took his breath away, followed by a deep blushing sense of shame. Who was he to admire a young woman? He was nothing.

He listened closely, heard the strange words falling from her tongue like silk.

A twig snapped.

Instantly she was on her feet, knees wide, bent forward, her eyes wild.

"It's okay. It's me, Henry."

She sagged to the bank beneath the willow like a crumpled piece of paper. She looked up at him as he approached, then asked hesitantly, "I am safe, no?"

He squatted a fair distance away. "You are."

"He is not my father."

"I didn't think so."

"I am from Delaware. I am Indian."

He caught his breath.

"By the . . . the, the shining . . ."

She spread a hand to the water.

"The sea?"

She nodded, a smile breaking across her face.

"Bad man take me."

"They? Or just one? How long?"

"One. Many times. I was . . ." She held up ten fingers, then only one.

"Time is long."

Henry understood her terror, her filth, her sadness, her wild eyes. Here was more proof there wasn't a God, at least not a kind, loving one who gave out blessings to everyone. Her suffering was far greater than his.

"Stay with me. My family," he said quickly. She shook her head.

"They come after me. Every time. Beatings very bad."

"They won't find you this time."

Almost, she was persuaded, but she went back to her vehement denial.

The river tumbled on, the hot sun creating silver highlights on ripples. The bees above the hawthorn bushes buzzed quietly as they sat side by side, gazing into the water, seeing nothing.

She continued drawing her brown fingers through her clean hair, humming low.

Henry said, "My home is upriver about two miles. Come with me."

She shook her head. "That was the way last time. They find every time."

"Then go back to the wagon. Stay there, till you have a chance to slip away. If they return tonight, go along upriver, then crawl off. They will think you're back there for many miles. The road follows the river. Before you cross another big hill. Please do it. You can trust me."

She turned her head to look at him, surveying him for a long moment, her dark eyes much older and wiser than her perceived years. Her face was round, dark and smooth, with almond-shaped eyes surrounded by thick lashes, a nose flattened against her face, a wide, full mouth.

A face that gave him so much pleasure, a sensation he had never experienced.

"Just let me stay here. To die, like raccoon, or squirrel."

"No, no. We want you to stay."

She shook her head. "You not know. Am dead now."

A strong urge to save her racked him. A desperation so great he felt it physically, in his chest, in his legs, as if he could run and run and run, then fly with her, take her across vast mountainous areas, across rivers and oceans, to a land that didn't exist.

"Look," he said urgently. "You must listen to me. After they get going, stay beneath the blankets for a while. When you feel the wagon going downhill, give it a few minutes, then jump from the back, find the nearest hiding place. The river is on your left. I will wait there for you. Our house is only a ten-minute walk east. It's the only one in the area. No one will see us."

She shook her head. "Die is easy. That is not."

He grasped her arm.

She jerked her whole body away, cried out, her eyes wide as she lashed out in her native tongue.

"I'm sorry," he said quickly, putting up both hands in surrender. "I won't hurt you. I don't want the men to have you again."

Slowly, she rose to her feet, her eyes on the river. Finally, she turned. "I do it. I go."

Together, they walked to the wagon and she clambered up over to lie on the dirty blankets, closed her eyes, and he went up to the barn and walked blindly from one section of the barn to another, without doing a lick of work. He went home with a bag of leftover pancakes, a few rinds of cheese, and a piece of pork, enough to make them a supper fit for a king with cabbage and onion from the garden.

Chapter 5

THE SUMMER MOON WAS LARGE, WHITE, AND mottled as it hung above the river, creating a path to walk across, a trail of silvery light disturbed by ripples in low places. The night wasn't dark, only shadowy, and it was warm. The silent swooping of bats and the call of katydids and crickets kept Henry company, sitting at the river's edge with all his senses alive, honed sharply to pick up any unusual sound.

For a long time, there was nothing, only the warm stillness and the moon overhead. An owl hooted, another answered. A whip-poor-will let out its call over and over.

Perhaps the two men had become too drunk to return. Perhaps they decided against traveling at night and stayed at the hotel. Or Lila had run away to die alone somewhere in the woods. He shifted on his uncomfortable rock, then held very still to watch a raccoon catch a crayfish, crack it apart, and wash each section carefully, like a fussy housewife.

The raccoon bounced off when Henry lay on his back on tufts of grass, his hands pretzeled behind his head.

The suspense was a thing he held in his hand, creating a tremble, the opening and closing of his fingers, the twitching of his thumb. He thought he might go mad, would go to the hotel and borrow a horse, chase after the men, overpower them both. If he would have a God, he might pray to Him about now, but he knew that if there was a God, He didn't hear the prayers of people like him.

He thought he might be sick with the suspense, the taut nerves that roiled his stomach and made him jumpy and irritated. He hoped no one missed him at home, the way he'd simply stayed by the river all evening.

When the light dawned in the east, only a lighter shade of dark, after the moon sank behind the ridge, he knew the night was over and her best chance was gone.

His eyes burned, heavy with sleep, his lower back was pierced by small stones, his face surely riddled by mosquito bites, but all of that was of no importance.

What had happened to her? Had they stayed at the hotel, or moved off in a different direction during the night? He had to accept the fact they might never see her again, no one at the hotel, but especially him. He started to regret he'd ever met her, the before Lila so much easier than the after Lila.

He got to his feet, made his way along the river bank before turning to go across the woods to his house. He entered the front door and went inside.

"Where were you, Henry?" his mother asked, but in a disinterested way.

"By the river."

"Mm."

"I'll sleep for an hour. Wake me, please Mom?"

"Will do."

He tumbled into bed fully clothed, fell into a hard sleep, and was rudely shaken awake by his mother.

He washed his face, ran a hand through his hair, and stumbled through the door on his way to the barn, without watching his step.

He recoiled violently at the crumbled skirt covered in blood, the black hair still tangled, the ropes on two wrists, bloodied and raw.

"Lila," he exclaimed breathlessly. "What happened? You're hurt."

He was wide awake, sitting on the steps, drawing her to himself, before the thought of cutting the ropes crossed his mind. His mother looked up, wide-eyed. "Henry?" she asked, but he was too absorbed to answer.

He cut the binding around Lila's wrists, threw them across the yard, before holding both her hands, palms up, bending his head to inspect the scraped flesh of her wrists.

"Tell me."

In halting English, she told him how the men returned late at night very drunk, falling over each other, finally collapsing beneath the wagon, promising an early start.

They saw that she'd left the wagon to clean herself in the river and designed a new way of security, tying her to the bed of the wagon with ropes. She'd chewed and spit endlessly through Bloody Run and beyond, finally breaking free at first light. She managed to get herself up and over the walls of the wagon, falling hard, rolling into a ditch. Then she was up and running, her shoulder on fire, the bruise through her thin dress throbbing.

Henry pieced together her story through gentle questions and her shaky answers. She'd run. On and on, through heavy branches, across rocks, and pushed her way through undergrowth with her hands held in front of her. Finally, she'd come back to a road. When a wagon came along, she wanted to hide, but she forced herself to ask for Henry Giovanni's house. The driver had told her the way. She'd stayed in the barn, not wanting to wake them.

"They must not find me," she said last of all.

His mother was there, taking it in with detached curiosity. Belle came, half-dressed and disheveled, and provided an agate pan of hot soapy water to clean the wounds.

One by one, the seven siblings, in various stages of undress, crowded around, mutely eyeing the girl.

Lila was grateful, then afraid, her eyes terrified of the surrounding forest, the sound of running water, a cry from one of the children.

She did not want Henry to go, but he had to be at the hotel. He restrained himself from telling anyone about Lila. He worked hard, stabled eight horses, and met a lively group from Millersburg, Pennsylvania.

Never had he been so anxious to get home, the ground falling away beneath his pounding feet, his breath ripping through his chest as he came through the door.

"Lila?"

"She's in the garden."

He stood at the edge, sweating and panting, a smile spreading across his features as she caught sight of him.

"I'm here," she said in a strong voice.

"You are. Oh, Lila," and he closed the space between them. She stood between the row of beans and gave him both of her hands, which he unthinkingly drew to his chest, bending over them as if they were a sacred gift.

"You're here. You won't be found."

"No. Not this time."

"We are poor. There isn't much for you," he said, as an apology to her.

"What?" She spread her arms to the garden, the surrounding forest, the river. "Everything here."

In the coming weeks, she taught them how to dry beans and corn, how to braid onions properly and to hang them in the attic closest to the fireplace. She caught fish in reed traps, large fish, in abundance, so that they were amazed at the lazy river's bounty.

She showed them how to erect a drying rack, how to clean and dry the heavy filets, how to hunt deer in much better ways, providing a steady diet of food rich in protein.

And Henry fell deeper in love, a newfound joy and abject misery. She was always on his mind, always an image of loveliness and beauty and every unnameable emotion.

His mother very wisely kept to herself, although she knew, which brought wave after wave of fresh sorrow for the man of her youth, the dashing Italian named Gilbert Giovanni, lost to the drink and Penny Shauf.

* * *

When the temperatures cooled and autumn nights turned chilly, the leaves began to turn scarlet, orange, and yellow. Catherine's sorrow lingered. She mourned not so much for her husband leaving the family as for the man she'd believed he was when they'd first met.

She didn't know if her parents were still alive, and that in itself created untold grief, as if she were mourning their loss, dead or alive. They were an ocean away and she knew she'd never cross back to her homeland. For a while, they'd written letters, though by the time they were received, many months had passed. At some point, Catherine stopped receiving any letters, and eventually, caught up in the struggle of daily living and ashamed of her family's situation, she stopped writing.

Lila was a blessing, yes, but it also brought a fresh reminder of all she'd lost—youth, beauty, love, the fleeting happiness she had in a former life.

* * *

At the hotel on the Juniata River, Charles took note of the spring in Henry's legs, the amount of work he accomplished in a day, the new color in his face, and light in his eye. When he sat in the drawing room with his wife, he mentioned this to her, thinking he'd receive a positive response.

She snorted. "What do you expect? The boy's all of seventeen or eighteen. They're so low bred, he's likely after Shirley. They're not far removed from the animals."

He took instant offense.

"Oh, but you know, my dear, that's very harsh, and rather heartless, don't you think?"

"Pshaw, Charles. I speak the truth."

"But he's a handsome young man. He knows more than I do down at the barn at this point. He's indispensable. I owe him so much more than his miserly wages."

"Mark my words, he's after something or someone."

She took up her embroidery and jabbed the needle viciously, the contempt evident in the set of her jaw.

It was hard to say when Charles had started to admire Henry. Much like his wife, he had always felt superior to the help. Those of a lower class needed a hard hand, must be made to obey by sheer power.

Henry had had his share of cuffs, swats across his back, and the yelling and belittling that went along with it. But like a good, well-trained horse, he kept improving, taking on more than his share of duties. He greeted newcomers affably, always as clean and presentable as was possible for those living in squalid conditions. The fact he was good looking didn't hurt, either, the ladies simpering and smiling. Plus, he got along well with the kitchen staff, which was unusual, the way Bertha didn't take kindly to everyone.

He figured Bertha was a bit heavy-handed with the bread flour, handed out extra from time to time, but it was alright with him, as long as his wife was unsuspecting. The boy had a tough row to hoe, with the family and all.

* * *

One afternoon, when the clouds hung low on the mountain and the air felt damp and chilly, Catherine was stoking the fire and feeling a weak kind of joy at the thought of the well-stocked wood in the lean-to on the south side of the cabin. To be warm, with food put by, was a blessing indeed.

She stopped, hearing an unusual sound in the yard. She couldn't imagine the intrusion, with the older children in school and Lila out deer hunting, faithfully intent on the food supply for the coming winter. Laying down the chunk of wood in her hand, she turned and made her way to the door before opening it a few inches to peer through.

She saw a bay horse hitched to a wagon, two elderly people sitting beside the swarthy driver, the horse obviously having drawn them a great distance.

She stepped out, mindful of being alone with small children. The elderly couple locked eyes with her, and dim recognition sparked into a question.

"Catherine?" the man croaked, his throat thick with emotion.

"Father?" she whispered to herself, before the unaccustomed tears rose to the surface. She stepped off the porch, held out a hand, as if imploring them, as if this extension of her body would make this scene true.

"Lady, I brought yer kinfolk." The swarthy driver grinned, yellowing teeth emerging through his unshaven face.

"Mother?" she asked, like the cry of a starving kitten confronted with saving sustenance.

She was at the wagon then, tears flowing freely, her thin, haggard face broken, a smile through the incredulous knowledge her parents had come after all these years.

The driver threw the reins, helped them down, and Catherine was in her mother's arms, babbling incoherently.

"Mother, mother," she whispered, then, "Oh, Father," and went into his arms, an incredible reunion of which she had dreamed so many times.

"Catherine, my dear. We've found you at last. Let me look at you," her father gasped brokenly. "The years have not been kind."

Her mother reached up to stroke her gray-white hair, saying, "Catherine, Catherine."

The driver heaved a trunk, wrestled it to the yard, followed by another, setting a black satchel beside on top. He waited as long as he could stand it while the greeting went on and on. He stepped up, cleared his throat, said he'd have to be on his way. Her father, taking stock of his situation, quickly reached for his coin purse and paid him generously, voicing concern for the horse.

"I'll just go on down to the hotel and rest for the night, before heading back. I thank you for the pay."

Doffing his battered felt hat, he sprang up on the seat, clucked to his horse, and was off, making a large circle in the yard.

The two youngest children darted out from behind the house and hid in the fold of their mother's skirts. Catherine reached down to touch the tops of their heads, gently removed them by a grip on their small shoulders.

Her mother was bent, shuffling her feet in the way of old age, her father still tall, but humpbacked, his long hair well below his earlobes, his untrimmed beard a shower of stiff white hair. Their clothes were plain, gray and black with no adornment whatsoever, but they would discuss this later.

As they went through the door to the shadowy interior of the crude cabin, her mother reached out a hand as if to enlarge it somehow. She stopped, turned her head to take in the surroundings, and gave her questioning daughter a look of the most tender pity.

"Catherine, tell me you had more room than this to raise your family."

"Come, Mother. You must sit down. I'll make us all a cup of tea. How did you ever find us?"

There was the long, crude kitchen table, benches, and a mixture of handmade chairs and stools. The kitchen stove, fireplace, dishpans on wooden pegs, a wood box, and a cupboard with two doors, a variety of buckets, cookware, and a straw broom. The remainder of the house was cluttered with beds, torn and motheaten woolen blankets, wooden boxes containing a jumble of clothes.

Her father took it all in, solemnly, the poverty and the neediness creating a dull ache in his chest.

They shared how they'd worried when they'd stopped receiving her letters and wondered together why she'd stopped receiving theirs. But then, mail at that time couldn't always be relied on. When they arrived in America, they came to the town she'd mentioned in her early letters and asked for her whereabouts. What a relief it was to find her.

Finally, her father asked gently, "Is Gilbert at work?"

Catherine had her back turned, scooping tea leaves into earthenware mugs, and he saw her shoulders stiffen.

Sighing, she turned, her face gray with sorrow.

"He has gone to live with another woman." Her mother's eyebrows lifted, a hand went to her chest.

"Were there troubles between you?" she ventured tenderly.

"It was the drink."

"God preserve us, Catherine. The drink? Tell us what happened. Tell us your story."

She brought tea, the slices of bread with the small brown crock of blackberry jam. Her mother watched the two pink spots rise on her cheeks, the evidence of lost beauty in the heightened color, the tired spark in her lifeless eyes.

"The years have not been kind, Lord knows. My Gilbert was homesick, despondent, took to the drink. I have birthed thirteen children, which have somehow survived. We made do. I wasn't able to provide for Gilbert the things he needed, and so he was forced to turn to the happiness he found in drink. He says I did not love him properly."

Her father's face showed no emotion, except for a flicker in his eyes, a set in his jaw. There was the slightest edge in his voice as he spoke. "I think, after thirteen children, there can be little doubt that you did your wifely duty."

"Well, yes."

"Catherine, you are not to blame," her mother said quietly, laying a blue-veined hand on her arm, the warmth of it a benediction.

"He says I am, and perhaps he is right. Look at me. I'm not the girl he married."

"He is a drunkard and an adulterer, and he lays the blame on his wife? I think not," her mother responded.

"We will pray for the well-being of his soul."

Catherine's eyes were hard as the anthracite coal.

"And to whom will you pray?"

Her father's consternation was evident in the sharp intake of his breath.

"Catherine, please tell me you haven't abandoned the faith."

"I'm afraid I have. You don't know how it feels, Father, to hear your children crying with empty stomachs, to send them to bed in such a manner. And yet they kept coming, these mewling, starving babies, my own flesh and blood, and Gilbert always glad to welcome them, never taking full responsibility of feeding and clothing them. And you speak to me of God? He has no mercy on the poor."

The door was flung open, a breathless Lila stopping in the rush to relay her news as she caught sight of Catherine's parents. Her eyes opened wide, taking in the black suit, the long white hair, the large white head covering of her mother.

Turning, she slipped out the door.

Catherine was on her feet, a hand extended, calling her name, but Lila was soon swallowed up by the surrounding forest.

"Have we interfered?" her father asked when Catherine returned.

"No. That was Lila. A young Delaware Indian from the eastern shore. She was abducted by two uncouth characters and is frightened of any stranger. She'll be back, I imagine."

She told them how Henry had met Lila at the hotel, had probably saved the girl's life. And how she, in turn, had taught them how to hunt, garden, and preserve food in ways they never had.

They listened, rapt, then her mother said, tentatively, "God's providence, no? How else can you explain it?"

Catherine didn't respond.

Her father spoke next, glancing at his wife. "We have joined the Anabaptist movement. I'm sure you noticed our different way of dressing."

"I thought perhaps it was just a style. I've heard of the movement, but I'm afraid I don't know much about it."

"We believe in adhering to a plain way of life," he answered. "Living apart from the world and all its frippery, our life carrying the cross of self-denial. Followers of Jesus Christ. We believe our baptism in the Catholic church to be invalid, as an infant at his or her baptism cannot know the way to the new birth, which is necessary upon baptism."

"Interesting," Catherine said, though she would have preferred to talk about almost anything else.

"Many who share our beliefs have suffered terribly. Things too awful to discuss." A dark cloud passed over his face briefly. "So we sold our land and buildings and have come to America to serve our Lord in freedom. We are well-endowed with earthly riches, and if you will have us, we will remain here with you."

Catherine couldn't fully absorb what they were saying. She was so used to her life of struggle, that any other way seemed impossible.

Just then the school-aged children appeared at the door, wide-eyed and hesitant, their faces apple-cheeked with the cold, their clothing in various stages of repair and discoloration.

"Come, children. You must say hello. Meet your grandparents from across the water," she breathed.

"Mother, this is David, Jacob, Sarah, Dorothy, and little Thomas."

Her mother rose to her feet and put out a hand to touch each one in turn, exclaiming at certain likenesses, admiring dark eyes, wavy hair, mentioning relatives as the children stood obediently. Her father rose to join his wife, his old face wreathed in a wide smile of instant recognition.

"*Ach*, my grandchildren. And what a blessing. What joy fills my heart on this day."

As he spoke, his eyes filled with tears of thanksgiving and joy.

Belle came home, her green eyes alarmed at the strangers in black, the youngest, Judith, perched on the old lady's knees.

She was introduced, her alarm turning to incredulity as she processed the arrival of grandparents, the glad light in her mother's eyes.

At suppertime, when her elderly parents retired to lie down before the meal was finished, Henry came home from his work at the hotel, found nothing amiss except Lila's absence.

"Where is she?" he asked, eyeing the trunks by the doorway, suddenly fearing the worst.

"Henry, please. My parents have arrived. Henry and Barbara Miller, from across the Atlantic."

"What? But where is Lila?"

"She came to the door, became frightened, and left. I went after her, calling her name, but she went into the forest."

His only reply was an agonized glance before turning on his heel and taking off across the lawn in a loping run.

Chapter 6

THEY GATHERED ROUND THE CRUDE WOODEN table, set with tin plates and spoons, no knives or forks. There was a vegetable stew with dumplings, bits of tender deer meat, stewed pumpkin, and baked apples with molasses.

Catherine hovered, apologetic, remembering dinners with silver knives and forks, crocheted tablecloths, fine crystal goblets filled with the dark wines of the European grapes. Oh, there was so much fallen by the wayside, her children sprouting like windblown dandelions caught in crevices of rock, to take root and grow like sturdy little trees, gathering nourishment where they could. Hardy, uncultured Americans, getting by with the plucky strength of their ancestors.

There was lively talk, becoming acquainted, then popcorn by the fire after dishes were washed and put away, her mother lamenting the absence of a sink and running water, Catherine smiling quietly.

And still Henry had not returned, not when the first star appeared at twilight, and not when the moon rose full and round over the jagged treetops. Catherine fussed, again apologetic, but shifted children in beds, leaving her parents to the privacy of their own room. She searched the windows, the doorway, for Henry's return, finally giving up and lying down beside little Thomas and Cornelius. Far into the night, she wept softly, neither understanding nor caring why, only aware of the blessed relief, the edges of her stone-cold resolve wearing down, leaving fissures of warmth.

* * *

Henry called and called, searched every spot he could imagine, then felt the pull of the stone arch of the bridge across the river at Juniata Crossing. He made his way to the hotel, cloaked in moonshine, the colorful leaves rustling in the stiff breeze, far below the sloping bank, the gleam of silvery water as it flowed to meet the Susquehanna, on its way to Lewistown and Harrisburg.

He slipped down the bank to the foundation of the bridge, the great stone structure formidable at night, every stone bathed in silvery light.

"Lila?"

His foot slipped in mud. He righted himself, caught the edge of the bridge, peered around the rough edges, hoping to find her in the spot where thick tufts of grass grew like an old man's moustache, heavy and dense.

"Lila?"

A low reply, and she rose to her feet, stumbling a little over the loose sharp stones.

"Is it you, Henry?"

"Yes. Come, Lila. We'll go home."

"I have no home." She turned away, gripped the bridge.

"What happened?" he asked hoarsely, reaching for her. He had to hold her, feel her body against his, an assurance.

She turned away.

"Lila."

"No. They are witches. Evil spirits."

"What? Who?"

"The old ones. In black."

"No, no. They are grandparents. My mother's family. They have come across the Atlantic. On a ship, Lila. They are here to stay."

"I go then. Somewhere else. They are black."

She held her face to her hands, shivered, ground her teeth with fear and loathing.

He wondered briefly about her beliefs, what she'd been taught as a child.

"White faces. Bad man and woman."

"Look, Lila. My face is white."

She shook her head vehemently, refused to look at him. He pressed his lips together to steady himself, then asked her to accompany him to the hotel.

"We'll ask if you can stay until we figure something out."

"No. Bad man come back."

"Then come home with me. Come on, Lila. Mother will be wondering what happened to us."

He reached out a hand. She looked at it, then slowly lifted her own and placed it in his. He closed his fingers around her small brown hand and drew her gently toward him. There were no words, only the gentle movement of the silvery moonlit water, the black silhouette of rustling trees and the stone mansion on the hilltop beyond.

She went to him, lifted both hands to his face and brought it to hers, her mouth warming under his as they both conveyed their need, the protection from hunger and slavery, from fear and cold and the abhorrence of greedy men filled with the spirit of evil.

His arms tightened involuntarily, and she returned the gesture, naturally, with so much to give, so much sadness and hopefulness. When they broke apart, she was crying, her face streaked with bright tears in the moonlight.

"I am no longer good."

"What?" he whispered, drawing her close again, stroking her dark, tangled hair.

"I am not whole."

Her whole frame shook against him, and he realized what she meant.

"You had no choice. The fact that you are strong, have not allowed your spirit to be broken, is an honorable thing. I respect you for your strength, and for your bravery. I love you, Lila. I would be so happy if you would be my wife."

He was trembling now, with fear of her refusal. She gave a small laugh, caught both his hands, and leaned back, drawing him with her.

"But we have no marriage hut."

He explained the need to be married by a man of the clergy, or a judge, the telling of their betrothal to friends and family.

"Why?" she asked, puzzled.

"It's just, well, how it's done."

"I will be your wife. Yes."

The stars did a happy pirouette that night, danced across the sky in the form of streaking comets and brilliant stars lit up for their joy. They made their way along the road to the house, her fears assuaged.

* * *

There was resistance, of course. Catherine said they were too young. Thinking of her own young romance and how painful it had turned, she wanted desperately to protect them from a similar fate. Plus, there were the practical considerations. If Henry and Lila got their own place and started their own family, how would she and the other children survive with no income?

As Henry and Barbara listened, the years of wisdom served them well, and they waited till both Catherine and Henry had exhausted their parrying.

Very solemnly, her father cleared his throat.

"Catherine, we have amassed a small fortune, a blessing from God through the rich soil of the Rhine river valley. Our crops and animals have done us a great favor, and your sisters and brothers have all been allotted their share of the inheritance. So now there remains a full coffer, and there is plenty, all glory to God and His ever-present riches."

Catherine watched her father's face, a puzzled expression developing by the vertical lines between her eyes, her lips pressed in anxiety.

"But you will need it. We have enough. We are getting by."

She wrung her hands in her lap, her head bent now, to hide the rising consternation. She had planned from one day to the next to keep her family from starvation, sometimes existing on acorns and watercress from the river. She simply could not fathom being offered a way out of poverty.

Her mother's hand came to rest on her arm again, as if her touch would have the power to get through.

"Catherine, there is much, much more than that. Your father wants to hire laborers to build you a house, but not here by the river."

Confused, Catherine began to weep.

Her mother placed a hand on her shoulder.

"*Ach*, my Catherine. The hardships you have endured."

"It is a gift. An inheritance. Our joy to make our children happy."

At this, something in Catherine gave way. For so many years she had held it all together as best as she could. Focused on survival, there had been little room for emotion. Now, the floodgates opened.

Tears poured from her eyes, and she would not be comforted. Her sobs finally frightened the children, and her mother took her to the back bedroom, put her to bed as tenderly as if she were a child, and stayed by her side, singing hymns very softly.

For two whole days, the family tiptoed through the house as their mother wept intermittently, releasing the years of pent-up hardship and devastation. Then she wiped her eyes, sat up, and ate. She drank clear, cold spring water, and looked around with fresh eyes. She extended a hand to Lila, called her "daughter," and began to plan a real wedding on the lawn that surrounded the cabin.

She dipped the quill pen in a pot of ink, and in a beautiful hand, she made out a guest list of more than sixty people. Henry and Lila would be married, after which the new house would be built upriver on a tract of land along the mountain. Henry would keep this cabin by the beloved Juniata River.

* * *

On a bright November day in Indian summer, when the sun shone like a loving blessing on trees still hoarding a few colorful leaves on stark branches, the wedding guests were seated on benches as the Baptist minister gave a brief homily.

Lila was astonishing in her white dress and veil, demure beneath the sparkling white fabric, so innocent and beautiful, her lovely dark eyes alight with happiness.

And Henry. What a proud young man, his strong shoulders clad in the first suit he had ever worn.

The vows were solemn—quiet, but meaningful—and Catherine wept, remembering her own vows to the handsome Gilbert. How could she have known the raging thirst he had already endured all through the day, the flask hidden beneath the marriage bed? Henry had chosen to exclude his father and the adulterous Penny Shauf from the wedding, to protect his mother, having no desire to see him on this happiest of days, or any day thereafter.

Charles Rusk insisted on hosting the wedding dinner, putting Bertha and Shirley into a tizzy, though they were also thrilled for Henry.

Charles's wife, of course, was reluctant, but waved her hand and took to her bed, telling him to carry on. She had never in her entire life thought she would see the day when he would bow low enough to accommodate the stable boy on his wedding day.

Bertha outdid herself with a large roast beef, sliced to perfection, potatoes mashed with good butter, black pepper and salt, fresh carrots dug from beneath their bed of straw and roasted in the oven, a cabbage slaw with winter radish sliced paper thin, pickled red beets and roasted butternut squash with brown sugar.

And the cake was a wonder, three layers frosted heavily with butter cream icing, golden and delicious.

Bertha's cheeks flamed with tension, her white bonnet slightly crooked as she screeched and yelled at the hired serving girls, wondering where Charles had managed to unearth such incompetence, while Shirley kept her wits together, moving from stove to table, filling in the gaps, silently calculating, seeing to things while Bertha screeched.

The tables were pushed back, the three-man band brought in, and the wide oak boards creaked to the sound and weight of couples dancing, weaving in and out, the light of the stone fireplace flickering as they swayed past.

Henry and Lila felt like they were dreaming, the happiness they were experiencing almost too good to be true, except that it really was. For all the times of pain and deprivation, this day was like a gift, an undeserved, bountiful blessing.

The grandparents sat on the sidelines, clapping their hands from time to time when the rhythm of the banjo and the guitar were especially catching. Their faith discouraged dancing and music, but they'd enjoy it today, having no desire to put a damper on such joy after all the hardship their daughter and her family had been through.

The stone walls of the grand hotel were sturdy enough to contain the festivities, every paned window gleaming with yellow light when darkness fell in the narrow valley. The Juniata River rolled smoothly on, around the base of the bridge, carrying a few leftover orange leaves beneath it, into an eddy where they swirled and stayed.

Chapter 7

Winter was in the sound of the wind, in the strength of the cold felt all the way to the bones, so building the new house on the tract of land beyond Bloody Run had to wait till spring.

Henry talked to Charles Rusk, and Charles suggested they could have the carriage house, which had not been in use for a few years. It was thrilling to tell Lila, who was coping with a lot of human beings in a small space with only colder weather arriving in the coming months.

She looked up from her embroidery, a detested task, but one she submitted to, Catherine's instructions taken seriously.

Every respectable young lady embroidered pillowcases, tablecloths, and handkerchiefs, so when confronted with an escape route, she took it gladly. They scrubbed and sanded, polished and swept, until the stone carriage house, which consisted of two rooms, was a perfectly cozy dwelling for the two of them.

Lila was easy to teach, learning the reason for sanding floors, for polishing windows, how to wash bedsheets and clothes in steaming agate tubs of lye soap and water.

Charles provided castoff furniture from the cellar, moldy chairs and table, an extra sofa from a bedroom, and so they set up housekeeping by the hotel. Henry rose early each day and took up his duties, managing the stables. Lila was never happier than being outdoors, traipsing along the riverbank with a net, scooping up a half-frozen catfish or rock bass, cooking them whole over a blazing fire, with steamed pumpkin.

The grandparents mentioned Christmas that year, celebrating Christ's birth, but Catherine drew her eyebrows into a straight line and said the children had never heard of Christmas until they went to school, and she'd told them it was only for rich people's children. Christ meant nothing to poor folk.

Her father gazed levelly at his daughter, said, "Catherine."

She shrugged her shoulders unapologetically.

Her mother felt her daughter's suffering and understood her resistance to religion. At the same time, she couldn't imagine letting Christmas pass with no celebration. She announced a few days later they would go to the butcher shop in Bloody Run and purchase a smoked ham, after which they would go to Gould's Confectionery and buy sweets for the children. This was their custom and they planned to continue.

In secret, they bought gifts at Landon's Mercantile—warm socks, scarves, flowered dress fabric, dolls, marbles, and a set of china dinnerware for Catherine.

On the thirteenth of December, the sky was the color of pewter, with a frosty wet air heralding a snowstorm from the northeast. Henry shivered as he stepped into the barn, thought it might be a humdinger the way the birds ate up everything he threw out for them. He'd counted fourteen cardinals, pecking at corn and the seeds from loosened hay.

Lila had seen a ghostly halo around the moon at night, a sure sign of snow, so she carried enough split firewood into the house to last a week. Henry laughed at her, but she said there was no harm in being prepared.

Sure enough, the temperature dropped, the wind picked up strength, and small icy pellets pinged against glass windowpanes.

The world outside became hushed and still, except for the sliding, whispering sound of snowflakes hitting surfaces, changing the drab landscape to a white wonderland.

Lila took it very seriously, stoking the fire, stuffing bits of rags into overlooked crevices, watching the firewood supply. There were no guests at the hotel in winter, except for travelers going short distances, visiting relatives for the holidays, so Henry was kept busy cleaning hearths, muddling up three flights of stairs with a bag of firewood on his shoulders.

He was on the second floor when Charles stepped out of his wife's bedroom, putting a finger to his lips and telling him to quiet down.

"Yessir. Beg pardon," he said, low and shamed.

There was only a brusque "See to it then," and he returned to her bedroom.

He felt every inch the chastened servant, knew he still was bowing and scraping his way into his superior's good graces, a dubious if necessary honor, after which he reminded himself he was an extremely fortunate young man, and never to forget it, either.

* * *

The snow came down relentlessly for two days, like a never-ending sweeping curtain of white, creating scenes of snow-laden firs, snowslides off the cliff on the opposite river bank, and the all-pervading calm and quiet over everything.

Henry and Lila strapped snowshoes to their feet to gather winterberry branches, spruce, and pine, toted it to the hotel in burlap bags, and deposited it in the kitchen, Bertha sighing and rolling her eyes at the snow melting beneath them.

Shirley served them mugs of wassail, and Christmas cookies with raisins and white icing.

"I get fat," Lila said, biting into her second cookie.

"Oh honey, you have no idea," Bertha yelled from the butlery, where she was rooting around for the container of cream of tartar for her sponge cake. And Henry stuck out his long legs, draped a foot over Lila's to warm it, drank the hot, spicy cider, and felt expanded, as if his world had righted itself, the pinched anxiety of times past let go.

He had come a long, long way from the misery and deprivation to this cloud of love and warmth and security. Sometimes he felt as if he should be thanking a being, a power, maybe a god of some kind.

But wasn't it rather silly to shout out, or speak, or whisper a thank you to thin air? Was there a real God, or wasn't there? He thought maybe there might be, probably, but if He was the kind of person who created the world, then filled it with sorrow and pain and hunger, it made no sense.

Lila said the Great Spirit that lived by the water dwelled in Delaware, but she wasn't sure if he'd followed her the whole way with the men who were not good. She shrugged, said it was hard to know.

* * *

A few days before Christmas, Charles came into the tack room where Henry was building a seat for the spring wagon.

When he sensed someone behind him, he straightened, ran a hand through his long hair, and raised his eyebrows. "Yessir."

"Hitch up the Belgians. I'm going for the doctor," he said in a hurried manner. "Be quick about it."

"Yessir."

He currycombed, brushed, fed, and watered them, and had just adjusted the traces when Charles stormed out of the house and down the steps, clapping a felt hat low on his head. He offered no information and Henry didn't ask. He kept on with his work and stabled the horses in the afternoon when he returned with a black-hatted man seated beside him.

He supposed it was his wife, and told Lila, who watched him with large dark eyes, but shook her head and said nothing.

"What is it, Lila?" he asked, hanging his coat on a peg by the door, then sitting on a kitchen chair to rid himself of his boots.

"Oh, not to say. You don't think like me."

"No, tell me. You know things."

"The wife is dying. I saw the white dove on the hotel roof yesterday. It comes for her spirit."

Henry shook his head, but caught her serious gaze, welcomed her warm body against his when she needed his embrace.

"Dearest, it's alright. You believe what you want. I will never make fun of you."

They sat together, her on his lap, their arms entwined, listening to the wind as the clouds scattered like torn wool, the gusts picking up, sending great walls of snow scudding through trees, racing along open fields. But inside the carriage house it was warm, a roaring fire on the hearth, woolen blankets on their bed, enough wealth and comfort for a king.

* * *

They took the cutter, a small sleigh built for two people, and the black buggy horse to his mother's house for Christmas dinner, the sun breaking through fast-moving clouds driven by a ferocious wind. There were huge drifts of snow along embankments, most of the river frozen across, with spots of open water in between. The black buggy horse seemed in a playful mood, rugged on the bit with a strong tendency to dash through deep snow, leaving Lila shrieking and covered in spray, Henry whooping with the thrill of it. They arrived before the dinner was prepared and divested themselves of their heavy outerwear, faces streaming with melted snow and red with cold. Catherine and her mother created a suitable fuss, ushering them in to get warm.

Henry's older married siblings all had their own Christmas dinners to attend, so it left only Henry and Lila, the grandparents and siblings, who were now seated around their grandfather who was reading from the Bible. He looked up, welcomed them, and invited them to listen. Belle had decorated with sprays of holly, ropes of pine, stars fashioned from yellow paper. It was all very pretty, and made the house smell wonderful. But Lila was drawn to the well-modulated voice reading the Christmas story, so she sat on the floor and drew Judith on to her lap, bent down and kissed her cheek.

She listened quietly, then said suddenly, "Why Herod want to kill the baby?"

"He was the Christ, and Herod feared for his kingdom."

"Like war?"

"In a sense, yes."

Lila nodded.

The grandfather kept reading and Lila kept listening.

"I miss the start," she said suddenly.

So the grandfather went back to the beginning, when the angel came to Mary and announced the good news. A few verses and she stopped him again, plied him with questions about Mary and why she had been chosen. Patiently, her questions were answered.

In the kitchen, Catherine was agitated, fidgety beyond the preparation for the Christmas dinner. She seemed to chatter unduly, to clatter cookware and stove lids, anything to drown out her father's words. Her mother put both hands on her forearms. "Catherine, I know you are struggling, but try not to resist the wonder of the Christ child's birth. You have reason to be hardened, but try to let it go, for today."

Catherine avoided her penetrating gaze, slipped out of her grasp. The subject was dropped, and the Bible story ended, keeping Lila enthralled. She told the grandfather she needed to learn to read, she wanted to read this story of a tiny baby born in a manger, to become God in Heaven.

She could feel it in her body—it was alive, this story, she told Henry before they sat down to the wonderful steaming ham.

His mother was fighting overwhelming emotion, trying her best to stay strong, to be festive for the children, but was, in fact, very close to losing her composure.

Only a few months before, she could not have imagined food in lavish abundance. The children cheering, clapping, their mouths wide as slices of ham were put on their plates beside mounds of sweet potatoes slick with butter and boiled cabbage and sliced carrots with applesauce and sour pickles—it still felt too good to be true. They had to be cautious, their young stomachs unused to such luxury, so they tried to eat slowly, remembering their manners.

The gifts were brought out, the grandparents beaming, the presents received amid squeals and shouts of delight.

Catherine put her hands over her face, shook her head from side to side, said, "No, no. It's too much. There are poor people who don't even have food."

But every item was unwrapped, the china dinner plates held and admired, the thin, delicate cups, the saucers and serving dishes, all in a pink pattern of roses and purple forget-me-nots. Gifts for the children, a quilt for Lila and boots for Henry.

Lila continued to feel a new sense of purpose as the day went on. She would learn to read, then decipher this strange story all by herself. Henry sat by her side, cherishing the sights and scents of Christmas in the old house, trying not to think of the times when it was less than a hovel, unfit for anyone to live in. And yet they had.

In late afternoon, there was a loud banging on the old wooden door. Belle went to the door first, throwing it open to two constables from the town of

Bedford, their horses' steam rising above their bodies like a smoke.

"Does a Catherine Giovanni reside here?"

Curt and to the point, they omitted all pleasantries.

"Yes, my mother."

Catherine went to the door, spoke quietly, then stepped back, a hand to her heart, another gripping the doorframe.

She was whispering to herself as she lowered her thin frame to the old sofa, but her eyes were wide and dry.

"He's dead." Her whole body shook violently. "Your father. Gilbert Giovanni is dead. Froze to his death. On Christmas Eve."

Her mother and father, although having left the Catholic faith, crossed themselves, her mother sifting her skirt through fingers accustomed to years of having her rosary beads.

"God have mercy on his soul," she pleaded to no one in the room, but to the One she knew well.

Her father's eyes were open wide, his lips moving in silent prayer.

The children gathered round, festivities forgotten as the sad news of their father's death was pondered. He had not been much of a parent, and yet he was their father, and they remembered the sober times, the times when he wasn't drinking, though they were few.

"Catherine, will you attend the funeral?"

"Who will pay for it?" was her first thought, which she voiced aloud.

"We will see to it. We will pay this woman a visit. And you will go with us."

Chapter 8

THE HOUSE WAS ON A BACK STREET IN BLOODY Run, wooden siding clapped on the fronts of rowhouses like rotting, crooked teeth, the stench of mud, horse manure, and cooking residue hanging over the narrow street.

Henry Miller adjusted his collar beneath his heavy, black coat and knocked, paused, and knocked again. The door creaked inward and a frightened face appeared, one that might have been pretty enough in former years, but was flushed and blowsy. She caught sight of the unaccustomed black garb, shrieked, and slammed the door in their face.

Patiently, he knocked again. The door slid open a thin crack and a hoarse voice rasped, "I know it's the devil come to git me. Go away, leave me alone."

"We want to talk about Gilbert."

"He's dead."

It was so cold their breath came in frosty puffs, the sun's thin warmth doing nothing to help, so

Catherine's mother asked if she could step inside to warm herself.

"No, you just go on down to the undertakers. It's warm in there. I ain't goin' to no religious service, so forget about me."

She stared straight at Catherine's cloaked face, her own registering a mixture of shame, hardened pride, and sorrow. But she said nothing and closed the door gently.

* * *

A handful of townsfolk, Catherine, and her family attended the service at the Baptist church, the plain wooden coffin open, allowing the congregants to pay their respects.

The tavern patrons shook their heads, murmured. "Poor old bugger. He was a good bloke."

Catherine and her parents, with all the children behind them, created quite a spectacle. For days, folks would ruminate about the row of nice-looking children, the proud way they walked, the grace with which they greeted the men who drank with him, as if they were all one, and one no better than the other.

But Catherine was the only one who shed any tears, mourning as much for the pain he had brought into her life as for the loss of the man she had once loved.

Henry lingered, trying to remember his father's face when it wasn't ravaged by drink. But he couldn't, and he found himself harboring bitterness, the turmoil of disgust and hatred inhabiting his soul. He was powerless to forget all he had suffered.

Lila took his hand, drew him away without speaking, and he followed her. But he knew he would carry this weight within for the rest of his life. It was a cold, hard sorrow no one could heal.

* * *

Work was slow at the hotel through January, the storms sweeping through the valley by a frigid north wind, delivering a foot of snow, then two and three, the wind creating drifts as tall as Henry. He stood, his breath coming quick and fast, as he leaned on his shovel to catch his breath, watching the array of birds dislodging snow from thick pine trees. Ravens called from bare branches, lifted their wings, and flew across the river to the ridge beyond.

Charles stepped out on the wide porch, drawing gloves over his hands. He stood, his face still, watching the ravens.

The early morning light was blue and lavender, the sun still behind the mountain, the air heavy with cold. The hotel was at its most beautiful against the backdrop of this stark mountain, the snow white and pure, the Juniata River frozen over, the water underneath dark and silent.

Henry was in awe of the workmanship, the great stone laid so precisely, the walls rising up four stories from the cellar, the deep porch facing the river below.

The many-paned windows glittered in the light, the wide-slatted shutters framing them. Smoke curled from the great chimneys, and Henry knew the fireplaces would all need wood, and it was his work to keep them replenished. He loved the hotel, loved his work, and found himself deeply grateful for all he had learned, and for Charles Rusk himself.

He had been harsh in times past, and was still an exacting presence, but underneath lay a heart of gold, kindness and well-being extended to his patrons.

"Hullo, Henry," he called out.

"Good morning, sir."

"You'll have me spoiled, shoveling everything open."

"I enjoy it."

Charles came down from the steps, his great bulk even bigger with layers of clothes piled on, his tall boots seemingly increasing his height.

"How is she?" Henry asked.

Charles nodded, his eyes alight. "She had a real good day yesterday. The cough has subsided somewhat, and she ate some of Bertha's noodle soup. As soon as the doctor can get through, he'll be paying us a visit."

Henry smiled, nodded his head, and went back to shoveling. Charles moved on, and the kitchen door was flung open, a spray of water thrown from a dishpan, then the door closed again.

The sun rose, filling the river valley with brilliant light. Henry squinted as he faced the great stone house, then held completely still as he heard the dull thud of hooves on snow. No one would be foolish enough to be out in this fresh snowfall, this debilitating cold.

Incredulous, he watched a team of two thin horses staggering across the bridge, drawing a flimsy wagon with a tattered canvas stretched over broken hoops. The wagon swayed and groaned, snow packed between spokes in the wheels, and a gaunt man with his hat pulled low over his face was huddled in a fur blanket, his face pale and drawn.

As they swayed into the lot by the barn, Henry stepped forward, a great pity welling up for the suffering creatures hitched to the wagon. He knew the snow increased their work significantly.

"Yessir," Henry said, stepping up to the team.

The man's eyes were like two dark holes in the cadaverous face, his mouth trembling like a truant child's.

"How do?" he said weakly.

"You need accommodations?"

The man nodded. "Guess I miscalculated. We aren't in a good way, my wife and children."

"Well, get down, you made it."

"We'll likely need to stay in the barn, young man. We don't have cash for a room."

His lower lip trembled like a child's, his face shadowed with gray, the heavy eyebrows drawn over tired eyes.

Henry watched the man but stayed silent as he shed the fur robe, stuck out a thin hand.

"Jonas Köenig. From Lancaster. We are on our way west, but snow and cold turned it into a disaster. Started too early."

The torn flap of the covered wagon was pushed aside, and a thin face shone from another fur blanket.

"Jonas, Levinia needs help," came in a rasping voice.

Jonas blinked, opened his mouth as if to speak, but closed it again and turned away. Henry looked the thin horses over, decided they, too, needed help and set to work loosening traces, unhooking the britchment.

Henry heard the quiet sound of footsteps on snow and the formidable figure of Charles Rusk behind him.

"What's going on, Henry?"

"Folks got started too early. Guess Lancaster County wasn't as cold. Sir, they have no money. I think they're sick, at least one. What should we do?"

Charles looked over the horses and the broken-down wagon with the bedraggled covering, the thin underdressed man attempting entry, the mewling sound from within.

"Poor buggers. Well, they can't come to the house. Not with Margaret's illness. Get Bertha and Shirley. You tend to the horses first, we'll get the cellar swept, fire started."

Henry sprang into action, leading both horses into the barn, steaming, emaciated creatures dying of thirst and hunger, their sides caved over protruding hip bones. One look at their hooves revealed the unshod foot streaming blood, the stench of decay and infection like a carcass in the summer sun.

Henry swallowed, blinked back tears. They would not have made it much father, no doubt.

The horses lowered their heads and drank greedily, then stood, quietly awaiting their fate. Henry knew if he hitched them back to the wagon they would both do their faithful best to keep pulling it as long as it was required. Faithful creatures, their loyalty to their master carried out day after day, in spite of painful hooves.

Henry led them to a box stall, gave them a fair share of oats, forkfuls of hay, leaned against a post to watch them eat, ravenous, their teeth grinding oats.

When he left the barn, the family was huddled in the snow. Shivering children, pale faces hidden behind enormous black bonnets, the boys with weather-beaten black felt hats and hollow faces. The mother, the wife of this man named Jonas, appeared to be nothing less than a ghost, her eyes lowered, her face having no expression at all, carrying the form of a child in her arms.

Henry went to her. "Come into the barn until we have the cellar prepared. Come."

Jonas went first and his wife followed silently, the line of seven small children behind them, all clad in black, all of them mute, frightened. Henry closed the barn door after them, said he'd be back as soon as he could, then hurried up the drive to the exposed cellar beneath the great wide porch.

Bertha was having a fit, breathing like a winded horse, muttering about the unfairness of life, and just what did that Charles expect from her, she'd like to know.

But Henry moved around her silently, knowing she was only blowing off steam, the kindly heart underneath. He swept the hearth of the great fireplace, laid the kindling, and started a crackling fire, then turned to carry in the firewood.

Shirley was sweeping and mopping the packed earthen floor, bringing down woolen blankets, old pillows. Oil lamps and candles flickered against stone cold walls, bringing a small degree of warmth.

After the crude wooden table was spread with a clean tablecloth, benches on each side, Bertha brought a reed basket of bread, milk and honey, a few utensils, while Henry ushered the threadbare figures out of the barn, taking notice of the children's red streaming eyes, the mottled complexions. He herded them through the heavy oak doorway, glad of the light the few windows could provide.

How well he knew this sordid desperation, the inner despair and shame, clinging to survival by a creaking, broken rope. Bertha and Shirley had gone back upstairs to avoid being exposed to the sickness, but Henry stayed, showed them the blankets, where they could lie down, then left to bring water in great, wooden buckets.

He returned to find the family huddled around the now roaring fire, holding out stiff hands, their faces impassive as the dancing flames cast light across them.

He turned to go, but was stopped.

"We thank you, kindly."

"Of course. You are welcome. If I can bring anything else, let me know. I'll be here all day."

"Yes. Very well."

As Henry went about his work, he eyed the great stone hotel in the light of the winter sunlight, the heaps of snow piled around it, and thought it was like a beacon, a light for weary travelers, holding out its arms for the poor, the wealthy, every class of mankind from everywhere across the states, but mostly those going west, that great beckoning destination luring so many adventurous souls.

It made him happy, being a part of it, proud to serve others who had met with misfortune, or like these Köenigs, simply miscalculating the elements, encountering illness. Clearly the horses hadn't been well fed even before they started out—the journey from Lancaster wasn't far enough to leave them in such poor condition, even with the storm. No, this family had been struggling long before they decided to head west. They were in no shape to attempt such a journey, especially this time of year.

He went to the carriage house for breakfast, told Lila about the travelers, her eyes widening with pity. In the morning light, her hair was sleek and shining, her skin like polished mahogany, her large brown eyes limpid with love and mercy. A great, consuming love rose in his chest. It was her face. He would never tire of enjoying her pretty face.

"I will go," she said, lifting her basket of herbs, the plants she gathered on her forays to the river, the ridges and ravines.

"No, Lila, please don't. You'll get sick. We have no idea what form of sickness they have."

She lifted a hand to stop him, made a snorting noise.

"I can heal. Not sick. Not me, Henry." She smiled, put an arm around his waist and drew him close, lifted her face to receive him, her beloved husband.

And his heart melted inside of him, as usual.

* * *

The odor of mildew and filth was overpowering as Henry and Lila stepped through the cellar door, most of the family lying down, covered in the fur blankets, the mother on a low stool by the fire, swaying with weakness as she tried feeding the feverish child, whose mouth was open, but no sound came from it.

A stab of fear sliced through Henry, but Lila stepped up to her, squatted down, and looked into the mother's eyes.

"May I have her?" she asked quietly.

The mother was beyond caring and promptly handed her over wordlessly. Lila carried her to the table, spreading the blanket beneath her, and Henry followed.

"Hot. Very hot," Lila whispered.

The little chest rose and fell rapidly, the mouth open, sucking for air, the fever racing through the limp form.

She sent Henry for a tub, swung the kettle over the fire as the mother deserted her post by the fire and collapsed on the fur robes with her children.

On his way back with the tub, Henry turned to see the carriage rumble past in the snow, relieved to find the doctor arriving to tend to Mrs. Rusk.

Inside the cellar, the father hovered.

Lila bathed the child in warm water, administered a poultice of leeks and garlic, rubbed the thin little feet with it, but the breathing became very shallow.

"The doctor is in the house," Henry said quickly.

"Yes. Could come see."

The doctor was packing his bags as he finished, talking to Charles in low tones, when Henry found him, quickly stated his business, and led him to the cellar.

There was nothing he could do, he told Jonas sadly. The child was well beyond recovery. He left, shaking his head as he went. In winter, there was

always illness and death, but it never became an easier burden to bear, and as he drove away, he allowed
himself to feel the weight of grief for the family he
left behind.

* * *

Henry hacked away at the frozen topsoil, swinging
his pick with frustration, trying to accept the death
of the poor little Levinia, who had gasped, greedily
sucking in tiny amounts of air until the strain on the
small heart became too great and she faded away in
her father's arms.

Life was cruel. The parents had been foolish. They
could have had the sense to stay home. Jonas was
limp as a rag, sitting there dry-eyed, stoic, holding his
dead daughter. Bitterly, Henry imagined him glad of
having one less mouth to feed.

A small service was held as the child was lowered
into the grave in the plot of land behind the carriage
house.

The father would not allow a Baptist minister or
any of the town clergy to administer last rites, saying

it was against his beliefs to be linked with the world, and read from a black hymnbook in a quiet nasal voice intoning the German words. There was no coffin, only the white rags wrapped around her, Henry wincing as the frozen clods of earth mixed with snow fell on the tiny corpse.

"The Lord giveth, and the Lord taketh away. Blessed be the Name of the Lord," he'd said softly, his wife by his side, nodding her head in unison.

They all filed back to the cellar, dependent on the kindness of strangers, this black-clad huddle of poverty from the county in Pennsylvania they called Lancaster.

And Henry's resentment grew at the stupidity of the starving man, the sheer cowardice, laying down any weapon of defense against bad luck, and simply taking whatever life handed.

This, exactly, was why he had no faith, and was not ashamed to say so. The world was unjust, unfair, there was no getting around it. His grandparents could believe the fairy tales they spun, but it made no difference to him.

The contention between him and Lila began with her learning to read, poring slowly over the Bible, one perfect, brown forefinger painstakingly following the words she gleefully deciphered.

One evening when the fire crackled merrily, she said, "Jesus nice fellow. He make man better."

Her dark hair shone in the firelight as she bent over the pages, her mouth sounding out the words.

She sat up and said, "I believe now. I believe."

Chapter 9

IN THE MONTH OF MARCH, AFTER A FEW DAYS of balmy, melting weather, when rivulets of water trickled out from beneath snowbanks and the threatening clouds lowered themselves over the mountain top, the ice cracked and boomed on the river. A stiff east wind began to blow, swaying bare black branches, sending the men hurrying from house to stable with hands clapped on their hats.

Around noon, the hard bits of ice began to slant across the river, creating a thin, undulating veil of white grit swirling on the ground, melting in open water, which soon turned any liquid into frozen solids. The wind howled down the chimneys, sending sparks across the hearth, flapped loose corners on the hotel, shivered the wooden slats on the shutters, tore rising smoke into shreds and hurled it to the northwest.

In the cellar, the Köenig family huddled together on their knees, thanking God for shelter and safety, all of them having survived the sickness little Levinia had not. They were grateful to have been allowed to stay here until their strength returned.

Upstairs in the great bedroom with the ornate wallpaper and the foreign, handmade rugs, a great fire sent warmth across the graying face of the burly hotel owner, as his wife, Margaret, lay dying. With him were a few scattered relatives, the Baptist minister, and his own memories.

She was buried in the church graveyard after the blizzard subsided, the funeral large and opulent, the ladies dressed in black finery, the men in black wool, bowler hats, and mustaches cleaned and trimmed.

Charles Rusk hosted them all in the drawing room, with Bertha and Henry presiding over the solemn groups serving plates of sandwiches and pie, small cucumbers, and sliced cheese. Charles was well known, a loyal friend and man of the town, so he was supported and loved by all who knew him. Childless his entire life, he felt the absence of heirs keenly, especially on this blustery March day, the day of mourning, the time when he realized profoundly the companionless existence now yawning open before him.

And Henry moved among the gentry, taking cloaks and hats, bowing, scraping, his gentle "Yessir," "Please, this way," fitting for a servant of Charles Rusk. He received many pleased glances from the ladies, a few flirtatious looks from batting eyelashes over hands held to giggling mouths, but his heart and mind were perfectly captivated by his one and only Lila.

After the last person had gone, the last carriage driven up the slushy drive on the road to Bloody Run and beyond, Henry and Lila helped Shirley clean up, remove chairs, dust the furniture, and stoke the fire before going to the kitchen to heat more water, steep cups of tea, and polish off an entire apple pie and the rest of the sandwiches.

Bertha was weary, anxious about her future without Margaret to tend to, afraid Charles would send her away, hire someone younger, more capable.

Shirley lifted her teacup, put it down again, swiped the back of a hand against her left eye, yawned, and said, "Get off it, Bertha. He'll never git rid o' the likes of yerself."

Bertha shook her head, cried great, wet tears for Margaret, and said no, he would. He'd get rid o' her.

"All this dying got to you, Bertha. You'll get over it," Shirley said, winking at Lila.

And Henry thought again how the sturdy stone walls of the hotel stood sentry over death and dying, the festivities of weddings, the gathering of destitute strangers, healing the sick, housing their animals, providing a means of living for the servants, all through one man, Charles Rusk, who now found himself alone and sorrowing.

The sun would tip over the top of the mountain, spring would arrive with birdsong and comforting breezes, and the stones of Juniata Crossing would welcome the new season.

The Köenig family decided to take up residence in a small brown house on the outskirts of Bloody Run, pay a small amount of rent to the owner of the apothecary, and Jonas would go to work clearing land for a wealthy landowner in the cove. His wife, Anna, would take in washing and ironing, and the children would go to school only a mile away. He offered one of the horses as payment for the month's stay, but Charles told him gruffly he didn't need more horses, he could give him to Henry.

Henry refused, saying he had not earned it, and Jonas shook their hands, loaded up their meager belongings and his family, hitched the well-fed horses to the repaired wagon, and set off for his new future as a hired hand, the West and its beckoning only a distant memory.

Charles Rusk turned away from the sight of the creaking wagon, wiped the mist from his eyesight with the back of his hand, squared his shoulders, and sighed. There was a man, penniless and having suffered the loss of his daughter, but still his quiver was full with children, a wife, a future. And here Charles was, completely alone in a great stone house, the hallways with the high ceilings echoing the tread of Margaret's footsteps, her voice, the essence of her being.

* * *

As the violets bloomed along the riverbank, the dandelions lifted their yellow faces to the sun, and Catherine's cheeks flushed with renewed will to live, buoyed by the company of her parents and the married children's frequent visits. Belle was growing into a young lady, and now the provisions were so plentiful, the fear of hunger and cold only a shadow on the outskirts of her mind, a reminder to be thankful.

Charles decided to paint and varnish, to repaper the walls, and to clean floors and windows to give new life to the hotel before the influx of guests would begin.

He sat on the steps, his great shoulders straining at the seams of his shirt, his graying beard trimmed and neat, his eyes squinted against the afternoon sun. His felt hat lay beside him, and Henry reclined on the steps below.

"So tell me, son, what you think. Do you know of anyone who could do women's work? The cleaning, washing floors, curtains, after the painters finish."

"My sister Belle could."

"Not Lila?"

"No, not her." Henry became engrossed quickly, scraping mud from the heel of his boot, and Charles caught the flush spread across his cheeks, thought *aha*. There would be a little one soon.

Teasing, he remarked, "Aw, you've been keeping warm in the carriage house, then?"

A slow grin spread across Henry's face, and he blushed a fiery red, reached back to slap Charles's pants leg, missed, and hit his thumb on the edge of a step.

Charles laughed, the first Henry heard since his wife's death, a sound he welcomed.

"Henry, my boy. I wish you the best. You know that. We've come a long way together, you and me. A more faithful worker I will never find."

Henry kept his face to the river. Praise was rare, especially from Charles, and he felt ill at ease. But his heart became alive, the blood in his veins fizzy with joy for the future.

* * *

Belle came to clean, Catherine driving her there in the light hackney her father purchased for this purpose. She needed a few things in town, and would go there after Belle was at work.

Henry greeted her warmly, his face lighting up at sight of her. He could barely believe the transformation in his mother. Her eyes were calm, but alive, the gray look replaced by vitality, a rose color on her cheeks. Belle hopped off, sprang forward on the heels of her feet, reached up to grab his jaw and give it a shake.

"Henry!"

"Hello, Belle. You're looking rather jaunty."

"And so are you."

They appraised each other, approved, and stepped back, smiling. They inquired about each other's lives, Catherine saying she must be moving along, before they were joined by Charles, on his way to the house.

"Good morning, Mrs. Giovanni. A pleasure seeing you again," he said, touching the brim of his hat.

She dipped her head in acknowledgement, answered in her quiet voice, "Yes. Good morning, Mr. Rusk. I trust you are in good health."

"I am."

"I think of your sorrow, with which I am well acquainted myself."

"Indeed, you are."

The look passing between them was shared understanding. She lifted the reins, said quietly she must be on her way, and both men stepped back, lifting hands in farewell.

Belle was full of her usual vigor, chattering all the way to the house, shown to her duties, and left to begin with buckets, mop, and broom.

She had never seen the upstairs of the grand hotel and tiptoed softly from room to room, her large eyes taking in the huge windows with ornate trim work, the high ceilings and freshly papered walls. She climbed ladders, washed windows and furniture, carried buckets of water up and down stairs, whistled and hummed low under her breath, made up fantasies about being a fine young woman in a fancy dress, with gathered sleeves and a low-cut neckline.

She became very hungry as the tall, dark clock in the hallway struck one, and went to find Shirley in the kitchen. She found her amid a stack of pots and pans, sauces dripping down the sides, flour and sugar scattered over the floor, and Bertha as red as a good sunset, screeching in short bursts, her breath giving out between the orders.

Shirley looked up. "Hello, Belle. You better get back up there. We have five, mind you, five parties arriving in two days. A messenger was sent. We can't possibility do it all, here in the kitchen."

"I'm hungry."

"Didn't bring yer lunch, then?" Bertha roared from the pantry before tossing her a hunk of bread and showing her the cheese. "Bring yer mum and yer lunch tomorrow. Me and Shirley can't do it."

The following day, Charles Rusk came through the front door on his way to freshen up after breakfast, having a meeting about another bridge across the Juniata River, and found Catherine on a ladder, washing windows in the drawing room, laughing at a remark from Belle. He stopped, amazed to find that sound coming from none other than Henry's mother, aged far beyond her years, living the hard life she had led. Harder, even, than he would ever know.

He could not bring himself to greet them, but crept past like a coward, without fully understanding his own motive. He hadn't asked for two workers. Would he need to pay her? He drove away, attended the meeting, and came home to a spotless house, the scent of soap and wax lingering.

He had never been lonelier, never felt the loss of Margaret and the children he never had more keenly.

There was Henry, but he had his home in the carriage house, and Lila, soon to have a child of their own.

Well, he reasoned, a man must rise above his circumstances, and this he would do, in spite of having to put all his resources into the effort. A believer, he knew there was a time for everything, and his faith would carry him through.

The wagons began to arrive, the first one late in the afternoon on a rainy day in April. The first was a sturdy team driven by a strapping young man, his wife bright-eyed and eager, perched on the wooden seat wearing a floral bonnet and a brilliant red dress.

Henry was kept busy for days on end and had very little time with Lila, who spent her days helping wherever she could at the hotel, content to be in the company of two women delighting in the secret of her upcoming birth.

Spring turned into summer, and still the wagons came, creating a rhythm of work for everyone, including Charles.

There was cooking and cleaning, laundry, ironing, always bedding to boil and scrape across washboards, gardens to tend, vegetables to clean, the list was endless.

Belle was hired full-time and assigned to the cleaning and washing, which she grew to love. Often, her mother would bring her in the light buggy, and sometimes she stayed if there was an especially large influx of guests.

Charles found Catherine late in the afternoon, bringing in the last of the washing in the backyard. The heat had been grueling, especially in the kitchen where bread baking had been done most of the day.

He stopped her, took the wicker clothes basket, and held it.

"You're working too hard, Catherine. I should have said something before, but I must start paying you for your time."

Her eyes were very green when she looked squarely into his. "I enjoy it," she said calmly.

"You do?" he asked, feeling a bit tongue-tied.

"I do. I have worked all my life, raising children, of which I'm sure Henry has told you there are thirteen. I'm sure, too, you know my life has never been easy, so now I enjoy helping here, for all the favors that have been done to me."

"Favors? I have never been aware."

"Then I imagine the kitchen help is who I should thank."

He understood then. He'd known, in a way, or at least suspected that Bertha and Shirley had given Henry extra food to bring home now and again. Unsure of what to say, he turned to go, still carrying the basket.

She said to his back, "We received many crusts of bread, potatoes, flour, oats. We would have gone hungry, had it not been for the charity from this hotel. Thank you, even if you didn't know at the time."

He turned back to look at her.

"I am glad of it. I wish I would have known—perhaps I could have done more."

She nodded, turned to take the basket, meaning for him to relinquish his hold on it. He kept his hands where they were, and hers closed over his. She felt the masculine hairs on the back of his large hands, the knuckles of strength, and dropped her own, the heat lingering.

They said nothing, only went their separate ways, the shame and reproach of recently buried spouses like a curse between them.

Chapter 10

When the heat dissipated into the fiery splendor of autumn, Henry rode the fastest horse to the doctor's office in Bloody Run, his words tumbling urgently, his brain scrambled with anxiety.

The good doctor, weary from a near sleepless night, sighed, hitched up his horse, and drove the six miles to the carriage house, where he spent all night with only a few hours of sleep.

Henry paced. He cried to the mountain and at one point beseeched the heavens to have mercy.

"If there is a God," he bargained in the end.

Exhausted, the doctor went for backup and returned with a midwife of the Lenape tribe, an ancient woman most people avoided. There was gossip of the old woman being cursed with witchcraft. Some said to enter her house gave you the willies for months.

There was a strong scent of bitter herb, there was lowing, singing, and chanting. Bertha kept a kettle boiling, wrung her hands, and prayed mightily, her great chest heaving with supplication and pleading. It was taking too long. Lila's strength was running out.

With the midwife tending to Lila, the doctor stepped outside for fresh air. Henry found him and begged to know what he could do to help.

"For God's sake, pray!" he said.

Henry was too much of a coward to tell him he didn't believe in a God who would actually help.

Just before the sun slid behind the ridge, Lila was delivered of a strapping son, a high crowned head and study shoulders, yelling with the capacity of healthy lungs.

Henry went to Lila first, tears raining down his browned cheeks, appalled at the state in which he found her, before turning to greet his son.

"He's a real warrior," Lila whispered.

And Henry laughed through his tears, grabbed the old Indian midwife, and pledged his undying love, then pumped the doctor's hand until he grimaced. There was Bertha, and Shirley, his mother and Charles, all a whirl of love and mercy and grace and family.

* * *

Lila named their son Joshua because she loved the story of Joshua and Aaron in the Bible. Henry said they could name him whatever she wanted, so relieved was he that both his wife and son were alive. He held Joshua and loved him, his love for Lila multiplied, even when he thought that was impossible, and gave the gratefulness to the doctor and the old Indian woman.

As winter approached and the miracle of birth had subsided, he began to experience an emptiness, as if the oxygen around him was depleted somehow. Lila watched it all and smiled to herself as she cared for their son, bathed him and swaddled him, fed him and caressed the small round cheek, brushed a hand over the thick, dark hair.

"Yes, my little warrior Joshua. Your strength will break down the walls of your father's heart, and he will believe in Christ. Let the trumpets sound, little man of God."

* * *

Catherine no longer moved through her days with the deadness attuned to extreme hardship, but the small seed of her parents' kindness had begun to take root. Her father, in his God-given wisdom and understanding, decided against the new house on acquired acreage west of Bloody Run, after seeing the bloom of youth on his weary daughter's cheeks after taking Belle to the hotel.

He felt the Spirit move within him, bowed his head, and whispered, "Thy will be done, Father."

Catherine said the house right here was all they ever needed. If they moved away from the river she would not be able to get a good night's sleep. She was so used to the night sounds of the running water, peepers in spring, bullfrogs and loons in summer, the booming and cracking of ice in winter. And was there anything lovelier than a shower of scarlet leaves floating on a moving current?

So they stayed, the old cabin renovated here and there, rooms added on, a pantry well stocked, a steer and two pigs in the barnyard, a roaster lording over his flock of anxious biddy hens. Roses climbed the side of the porch and geranium seedlings from a neighbor grew along the front, but when winter arrived, they were set in coffee tins and placed on the deep windowsills of the kitchen.

Catherine thought of the depth of their former poverty at times, the dwindling of her youthful faith. She had become embittered, she knew, and wasn't ready to trust God just now, either. Things were better, yes, but she knew pain or tragedy could be right around the next corner.

She heard her father read the story of Zechariah in the temple, the man to whom a son had been promised, the forerunner to Jesus. Now how was that old man expected to believe he would have a son? Some of these things were a myth, likely, she thought to herself, as she clattered dishes in the dishpan to drown out the sound of her father's lovely old voice.

She knew these Bible stories. She had been raised in a Christian home, for sure. It was just so hard to believe now. But perhaps someday she could.

* * *

Christmas would be coming soon, Catherine thought to herself as she turned the page of the calendar. She looked forward to it, this year. There was much to celebrate, even without thinking about the birth of Jesus. And for the first time ever she would be able to buy gifts with the money she had put away. Charles had insisted on paying for her time working at the hotel. She would buy peppermint candy for the children, socks and yarn for her mother, and she'd find a toy for her new grandson. She would bring in great swatches of juniper and spruce, pinecones, and chestnuts, and bake a great sponge cake with brown sugar icing.

Should she invite Charles? She was keenly aware of his loneliness. She blushed all alone in the pantry, thinking of their hands on the clothesbasket.

But time had passed, hadn't it?

* * *

Charles Rusk sat in the blue wing chair by the fire and stared into the leaping flames. Around him, there was total silence except for the creaking of wooden shutters occasionally, or the sound of roaming coyotes down by the river. To say he missed his wife was an understatement. He missed her with the aching void that seems to be the lot of all grieving humans. She had been the great love of his life, but had become bitter over the years, childlessness spreading through her like a disease, causing her to become sardonic, stinging.

But he forgave her completely, God rest her soul. This great hotel, this house in which he lived alone now, seemed dispiriting. He thought of times past, his rough ways with Henry, the faithful women in the kitchen, the brash manner he'd often exerted over his guests.

He would make up for those times.

He sat up, then rose to his desk for paper and his quill pen. He would plan a great Christmas party in honor of his faithful servants. There would be singing and caroling, and wassail, a great smoked ham, a true celebration of the Christ Child come to earth.

* * *

They chopped, split, and hauled wood, repaired broken mortar between stones, replaced a porch post and insulated barn windows with newspaper and rags. They hauled manure when the ground froze, and Charles told Henry of his plans. Henry rode over to tell his mother and grandparents, the children jumping up and down, Belle's cheeks flushing. She would get her friend Sally to help her with a fashionable new dress, pay for it with some of her wages.

Lila grabbed Henry's hands, swung him around to the tune in her head, and Joshua laughed out loud.

Bertha's eyes snapped and crackled, said she'd make it the best Christmas party ever, and set to work making peanut brittle the following day.

So much anticipation, so much joy. It became infectious, and Henry found himself swept up in the spirit of Christmas, sitting by the fire at night holding his small son, staring into the fire as he thought of being delivered from his former life of misery.

He had done nothing to deserve such a hard start in life, but also didn't deserve all the blessings that had come his way. For so long, bitterness had left him rotting from the inside out, and he felt his own putrid sin. How could any God look down on his wretchedness and fill him with any goodness? Lila, his son, Charles Rusk, his work at the hotel . . . all a gift. Especially Lila and Joshua.

If he lived to be a thousand years old, he would never deserve them. Was life all just chance? Or was Lila right when she spoke of God directing their lives, even through hard times? He was so grateful and yet also felt unsettled, though he couldn't put his finger on why.

* * *

Candles were crafted in the kitchen, Lila bouncing Joshua to put him to sleep as Bertha melted wax on the stove. Shirley was mixing gingerbread cookies, singing at the top of her lungs, then dissolving into giggles.

The mantles would be filled with candles and evergreens, holly and ivy, red apples and chestnuts. Oil lamps everywhere, hung like chandeliers. The rugs rolled up and put away for the dancing. A live band. They were inviting the mayor and the town council, but the guests of honor would be his staff and their families.

* * *

One night, when her father finished reading to the children, Catherine felt as if she had arrived somewhere, having no explanation for this soothing sensation, except for the fact she needed to hear her father read more of the story. So she left her dishtowel on the dry sink and sat on the rocking chair, her lap instantly filled with little Judith, who gazed up into her mother's face with a rapturous love.

And she knew. As sure as the sun rose in the east and settled in the west, she knew Christ was born, for her.

He lived and died for her as well as anyone who believed. God, His Father, raised Him and it was finished when he ascended into Heaven. It was all true.

Her father's voice filled her soul. She absorbed his words greedily, like a dying man who receives a drink to save himself. She wept softly, and her eyes shone like the Christmas star itself.

Later, when the children were in bed, her father asked her very gently if she had felt the power of the Christmas story, the way her eyes had been shining like the star in the east itself.

"Ah, Father, indeed. I have been finding hope in bits and pieces along the way, so I must have been opening my heart without knowing. So much bitterness and sorrow over the years with Gilbert, God rest his soul. My life was hard, and my heart turned to stone against God. I felt he didn't care about me and the children, the hunger and cold, the raw face of poverty threatening so that I thought about ending my life in the river. It was only the thought of my hungry children that kept me from it."

She raised eyes of tortured memories.

"Healing and hope have slowly found their way in small changes, my heart finding crevices and openings, so it must be God cares, whether we accept it or not. Somehow, Father, the words you read are glittering with meaning."

Her father's eyes were misty as he placed a hand on hers.

"My daughter, it is the work of the Holy Spirit, the Comforter He promised us. My old shoulders have just been relieved of a great burden, and I shall go to all the Christmas celebrations with overflowing joy."

The following week was a flurry of activity as they readied the old house by the river for Christmas. Swept and dusted, mopped and polished, the rooms held the wonderful aroma of soap and wintergreen, spruce boughs and holly with perfect berries.

Her mother was in the kitchen with her, applying the rolling pin on rounds of pie dough, the mincemeat and molasses in a bowl beside her, a song tumbling from her mouth, like water spilling gently over rocks.

"The first Noel, the angels did say.

Was to certain poor shepherds in fields as they lay."

Catherine looked up from mixing eggs and sugar.

"You think the shepherds were the first to know, Mother?"

"Yes. But the wise men in a faraway land were searching the Scriptures as well, and who knows how many others? Oh, it's such an amazing thing, Catherine. Here was the world, waiting on the Messiah, their heads filled with the earthly version of a wealthy kingdom He would establish. It's almost more than we can comprehend, so the Holy Spirit must move our hearts to grasp it all. Here was a poor couple come to pay taxes, no room in the inn, and the infant, the Messiah, was born in a stable. A stable, mind you, Catherine. And no one knew it was the Messiah, save for a few, until the bright angels told the shepherds. Shepherds were not held in high esteem, in those days. Crude, poor men of low degree, simple in heart, but it was to them the blessed news was revealed."

"Do you think Mary knew?"

"I do. And Joseph knew, but I imagine the shepherds coming to worship Him helped their own belief that this Child truly was the Messiah."

Catherine stirred brown sugar and water, set the cast iron pot on the cookstove, before opening the lid to add a few sticks of wood.

"Mother, if I really think about it, we have our own Christmas miracle. No one could have told me how my own beloved parents would come across the Atlantic, my life restored in so many ways. What have I done to be lifted from the agony of my existence with a man in the grip of alcohol, God rest his soul?"

"The courage and strength you possessed without faith in God, when times were bleak, is more than I can comprehend. Words fail me."

"Almost, I didn't survive. You know that," Catherine whispered softly.

The sponge cake was tall, and as light as they'd hoped, filling the old cabin with its sugary aroma.

Outside, the winter sun lost its strength as graying clouds set in, and the wind rustled through bare branches, sending a few brown oak leaves to the ground, shifting fir tree tops and rustling spruce branches.

Catherine's eyes shone as she lit an oil lamp, eager to see the falling of Christmas snow.

Chapter 11

SHE SENT DAVID AND BELLE WITH THE OLD horse hitched to the repaired cutter to the hotel, with a sealed envelope for Henry and Lila, one for Bertha and her husband, one for Shirley, and finally, after many moments of doubting, one for Charles Rusk, who smiled when he opened it and read the invitation written in a fine hand on thin parchment paper. The party at Catherine's home was to be a few days before Christmas, and the party at the hotel would be on Christmas Day.

The second snow of the season was coming down as they all piled into the heavy bobsled with two extraordinary Belgians hooked to the doubletree, the black harnesses gleaming with a fresh rubbing of linseed oil, the silver manes and jingling bells shining in the white light. Henry drove, with Charles on his left, high up on the front seat, the rest of the group wrapped in woolen blankets with hot bricks at their feet.

Henry called to the horses, knowing the drive was uphill, and was rewarded by the lowering of great muscular haunches as the wide feet dug into the snow, drawing the heavy bobsled up and over.

Lila's face shone from the fur-trimmed hood of her coat, her dark eyes snapping, her teeth white against her brown face, relishing the pure air, the wonder of being out in the elements, her son bundled away from the cold and the biting wind.

Bertha's scarf was tied around her mouth, only her red forehead and small eyes visible. Her husband Dan sat like a giant stump, his felt hat drawn over his eyes, his coat collar concealing the remainder of his face.

Shirley sat in her red cloak, wisps of blond hair from beneath it, turning her face to the wind and saying wasn't this fine, being out and about like this, already celebrating Christmas with a real party, which Lila echoed right back. There were gifts for the children, coffee and tea for the grandparents, a fine shawl for Catherine, all wrapped in brown paper with pine boughs and twine.

* * *

They were met at the door by the father, with Catherine behind him, her cheeks flushed with heat from the cookstove, the burgundy dress with a white apron tied over it bringing out the color even more. There were greetings, handshakes, a flurry of small hands reaching for the baby Joshua, wet scarves and coats hung on pegs behind the cookstove.

The house was small, with low ceilings, but there were oil lamps and plenty of candles, a table spread along the middle of the largest room, which could only seat twelve, but the children ate in the kitchen, so there was room for everyone.

Charles paid no special attention to Catherine, but sat with Dan and Henry, listening to her father's tales of the old country. He shook his head at the thought of all the religious oppression, the breaking away from the Roman Catholics and the ensuing persecution, families cast into prison, losing their homes.

Dan pondered the Anabaptist movement, questioned the need for plain clothes, which Catherine's father he explained in detail. They were saved from argument by a call to the table.

In the light of a dozen candles, the snowy, gray day providing a minimum of light through the small windows, Charles found himself a big oaf, bumbling, his fingers like sausages, helplessly unable to keep his eyes off Catherine, whose face was glowing, her green eyes like the first leaf in spring, like deep pools by hanging fronds of ferns. He found himself becoming poetic, then ashamed of his own thoughts, suddenly extremely amorous but absolutely tongue-tied.

She had lived a life of unspeakable hardship and suffering, delivered of thirteen children with every available penny going to Gilbert's burning drive for alcohol, thin and weak and bitter. This was the thing he could never forget, the sheer amount of courage to live on, day by day, denying her husband nothing in spite of the ill treatment.

She was too good for the likes of him, but even as he told himself this, he planned on the ring he would buy.

The food was simple, but delicious. There was a ham, smoked, baked, and sliced, falling off the bone in salty slices, mounds of mashed potatoes with brown butter and rich ham gravy, mashed turnips with parsley, carrots and sweet potatoes, all from the garden, all put away for winter, a luxury Catherine could not have imagined a few years ago. The maple sponge cake with brown sugar icing was applauded with clapping and cheers, the mincemeat and shoofly pie eaten in big, tasty forkfuls.

"All we need are canned peaches, which seem to be only a dream from the old country," her father remarked.

"We have more than enough as it is," Catherine answered. Henry watched his mother's face and barely recognized her. It was as if a dried flower bed had come to life, colored and bloomed beneath his eyes.

He felt the sting of tears and lowered his eyes.

They all lingered over cups of coffee, the conversation flowing freely, except for Charles, who was strangely distracted. The children all ran out to play in the snow, and the women did dishes before retiring to the chairs taken away from the table, Catherine in her rocking chair by the fireplace, with the smallest child on her lap.

Dan was holding forth about the new bridge being built across the Juniata, the waiting on the town council, and the sheer necessity of it.

Bertha's eyes snapped, and she moved one foot over the other as she smoothed her voluminous skirt over her rounded stomach, her chest heaving below the pearl buttons.

"Progress. Everyone yelling and clamoring for progress. I say let well enough alone. You want to cross the river, come on up the road till you get to the hotel and cross the river. We've always done it. Before that, you drove across and hoped to high heaven you'd make it."

A wide smile creased the old man's face.

"Well spoken, Bertha. Except for spring floods, of which I am assured there are plenty."

"There sure are," Dan shouted, raising a hammy fist.

"Remember the one in March of '89? 1789, that was a year we'll never forget. That was when Wentzel Hardy's load of cattle went over, cows bawling, wild-eyed, drowning one by one, old Wentzel clinging to a beechnut till his fingers nigh froze. His hair turned white in a day's time, almost lost his mind with fear, that brown river rolling along inches below his backside. Hung there most of the day, I tell you. They tried to tell him, so they did, but would he listen to reason? Nope. Had to hang there for hours whilst all his cows drowned."

Bertha leaned forward, slapped what was left of her leg after her stomach was arranged over it.

"That was only a day or so after Calvin Hershy went over, lost his horses, wagon, and his own foolish life. His widow mourned the rest of her life. Wore black no matter the season. Always black. You have to respect a river after it rams for five or six days straight."

Dan took up when she left off.

"Flooded half of Bloody Run, too, that year. I mean, the Juniata starts to turn brown, churn right along, you best get out of its way."

Henry sat listening, thinking how Dan and Bertha spoke fine English among company, but a country pidgin when working at the hotel. He grinned to himself.

What would he have done without Bertha in the hotel kitchen, saving scraps of food meant to fatten the hogs?

So much kindness to an unknown starving boy, a servant barely able to stand on his feet with the hunger.

He bounced little Joshua on his knee as he listened to the entertaining stories, revolving around the river and its town, the local people inhabiting the houses still being built.

Good people, with solid upbringings who sat in the pews of the many churches and worshipped God, most of them, and he proud to be among them.

Soon, he would take Lila to church like she'd been asking for. Some day soon.

* * *

They started home late in the afternoon, the gray clouds torn apart to the west by the force of arising wind moaning through fir trees west of the cabin.

Charles looked up, pulled his gray felt hat down over his ears, told Henry they better make a run for it. The way this wind had started howling, soon they wouldn't be able to see a thing.

Obedient, Henry brought the reins down, called a lusty "Hi-yup there!" and was rewarded by a surge of speed, the wide runners of the bobsled shushing through heavy snow.

The wind at their backs, it was smooth going, till the wind picked up to a ferocious roar, sending great billows of snow like a solid curtain of white across the sled and the horses, obliterating everything in their path.

Henry drew in on the reins, his feet propped against the dash for leverage, instinctively recognizing the danger, just before the horses spooked at a shadowy figure and ran the bobsled up an embankment. A yell from Charles, a shriek from Bertha, and the whole load was deposited onto the road, floundering in deep snow as the Belgians came to a halt, the wagon twisted on its side, the tongue and double-tree poked up at a dangerous angle.

The wind whipped the snow and threw the horse's manes and tails into disarray as they stood patiently, waiting on orders before they proceeded.

Henry's first concern was Lila and Joshua who were seated quite comfortably in a snowdrift, Lila laughing uproariously as she pointed a finger at Shirley, who lay on her back, calmly creating a snow angel by moving her arms and legs, Bertha on her hands and knees, trying her level best to save her dignity by getting out of this humiliating situation by herself. Dan lumbered through the snow, unhurt, to help his rather portly spouse to her feet, then let out a stentorian guffaw, his giant frame rolling with the nonsensical scene before him.

But Charles and Henry were occupied, unhitching with difficulty, turning their faces away from the clouds of driving snow, recognizing the danger of the four or five miles left to go before reaching the hotel. Dan, Shirley, and Bertha would have to stay for the night, whether they agreed or not.

After righting the wagon with heavy branches and everyone's heaving, they were back on the road, Henry doing his level best to peer through the driven curtains of snow. A wide area without trees was the worst, but with everyone's eyes peering through, calling directions, sections of the road going through thick stands of spruce and pine, they traveled safely a few more miles.

Twilight crept across the land, turning the clouds of driven snow into blue shadowy specters.

Charles yelled at Henry to let the horses find their way, his eyes squinting from beneath the brim of his hat.

"Think it's the best way."

The minute Henry loosened the reins, the horses lifted their heads and surged forward. Wet and cold, the group on the bobsled bowed their heads to the howling gale and shivered, finally praying to arrive at any shelter for safety. Joshua cried, his feeble whimpers tuning to enraged yells of cold.

On they went, the great Belgians running in perfect unison, the jingling of bells and dull thwacking of massive hooves on snow heard faintly above the shrieking wind. Henry tilted his head to peer at Charles, who merely nodded, bringing his gloved hand to a forwarding motion.

He recognized the incline on their way to the barn, the dark silhouette of the hulking hotel in the gloom. He said thank you to the sky, and meant it.

Shivering, wordless, so relieved to be by the barn, they all made their way to the hotel to stoke fires and get the kettle boiling, while Charles and Henry saw to the comfort of the horses.

They struggled to open doors, struggled to close them again, but finally in the quiet of four walls around them, they patted the great Belgians' necks.

"Good old sods, these two. Never seen better. Like you, Henry, always obedient, which may have saved us all. You're a good lad, son."

Henry didn't know what to say to praise, never had and likely never would, so he dipped his head and busied himself, forgetting the thank you entirely.

"You need me to help with the fires?" he asked, as he ran a dry burlap bag over the steaming horse.

"Dan and I will see to it. You take Lila home, see to your family. No need to get out early, the way this is blowing, we'll be snowed in good and proper."

With Joshua's cries to guide him, he caught up to Lila and hustled them into the safety of their small home, Henry settling her on the rocking chair with extra blankets while he rekindled the fire. Joshua nursed greedily, and Henry searched Lila's face to gauge her feelings.

She was smiling, but there was a pucker between her eyebrows. Finally she said, "Henry."

"Yes, Lila?"

"White men never understand. Woolen not good like the skin of bear and deer."

Henry stood, looking down at her, thinking how he would never tire of her face, that perfectly contoured brown face with symmetrical features he loved so much.

"You're saying outerwear made from the skin of animals is warmer?"

"Yes."

"Why don't you make them?"

"And snowshoes. I do. I make them."

"Sure. You do that. Did you enjoy Christmas with my family?" he asked, reaching down to lay the back of his hand along the contours of her cheek.

"Yes. I enjoy."

That night, as they clung together in their cozy bed, the wind lamenting and wailing around the carriage house, Henry was taken by surprise at the welling of gratefulness in the core of his being, what he supposed was his soul.

Was God like a refuge? Was he like four solid stone walls that kept you from fear and life-depleting anxiety?

It was warm and safe and quiet here, this night when the elements were fierce, when they'd traveled safely through the howling winds.

Lila said sleepily, "Charles Rusk awful quiet. He likes your mother. They will marry soon. Be happy like us."

Chapter 12

On the night of the big Christmas party at the hotel, Bertha was red-faced, exhausted, and jubilant. She grabbed Shirley by the waist, cocked an elbow with her knuckles on her hip, and did a wobbly two-step.

"Indeed, love, 'tis fit for a king, this grand food. The sponge cake is high, the pies are flaky, stuffed full of apples and wild berries, the lemon tart is perfect, the ginger cookies crackling and chewy, the roast of beef melting on yer tongue, I'm telling you."

She grinned mischievously. "Let's watch them arrive. We'll open just a hair, the kitchen door."

The mayor arrived, his beaver hat piled on his head, his short, portly figure like the gait of a black bear. No matter how many airs he put on, he would always wish for more height.

"Short and fat as a pink pig," Bertha hissed.

The town council, five men and their wives, dribbling through the door in all manner of finery, fur hats, muffs, woolen cloaks reaching from neck to floor, fancy gloves, faces showing no sign of the cold through layers of powder.

And the dresses!

The hired maids helped the ladies with coats, hats, and scarves, brought trays of tiny cookies and sandwiches, offered tea, wassail, beer or rum mixed with it.

Bertha kept an eye on prepared trays, dashed back to the spy hole, kept up a running commentary on faces and styles, with Shirley in stitches.

When Henry and Lila arrived, she sighed, her eyes going watery.

"Now there. There, Shirley. Them two's the best. Look at 'em now, do."

Lila in deep red, the color of ripe cranberries, a row of black buttons down to the V-shaped front, a wide neckline with her black hair in a smooth French knot. Henry beside her, regal in his black suit, the white collar rising above it, little Joshua whisked away by the hired nanny.

"Right proud, ain't we now?" Bertha whispered, and Shirley nodded, said yes, she was.

Then the grandparents, regal and dark, their white hair and pale skin like saints, their eyes taking in the staircase, the papering and array of lights.

Catherine, then, in pale pink, her reddish hair mostly gray, but a youthful blush, a flash of green eyes as Charles Rusk held her hand far too long.

"Ah, we'll have us a new mistress, Shirley, you mark my words. This grand hotel will be filled wi' the sound of children."

She had planned on saying more, but choked up on the words, became irritated, and told Shirley to check the fire in the cookstove.

* * *

Charles announced the evening meal and the guests moved forward, found their cards on dinner plates, and were seated.

Catherine found herself to the left of Charles. It took every ounce of composure to keep her feelings in control. She didn't dare to look at him, so distinguished in real evening clothes, so way out of her lowly stature.

Henry and Lila were to his right, then the mayor beside Lila, the five members of the council, an assortment of friends. The children ate upstairs in the nursery, with the nanny who was hired for the evening.

Charles asked everyone to hold hands around the table while he said grace. All hands reached out. Heads bowed, as Charles prayed for the gift of the Christ child, for food, family, and friends. For purity and grace, with Catherine's calloused, slim fingers in his.

There was a fragrant onion soup, with tiny triangles of buttered toasted bread. Red wine and white wine, charmingly denied by Catherine's parents, whose faith did not allow it. Beef roast, mashed potatoes, sweet potatoes, baked corn, and shredded cabbage with a vinegar dressing. Bertha's Pennsylvania Dutch noodles with brown butter.

Catherine was hesitant, felt out of place, tried her best to remember proper etiquette, would not look at Charles till he addressed her by name.

Carefully, she laid down her fork, turned her head to find his eyes on hers, a graceful move he found exquisite, fitting for a grand dame.

"Do you enjoy the food Bertha prepared?" he asked. She smiled, gave a slight nod, and lowered her eyes.

Charles turned to Henry and Lila and complimented them both, with Catherine looking on. Conversation flowed around them, wine glasses were filled and refilled, the portly mayor turning an alarming shade of pink, inserting a finger into the increasingly snug neckline from time to time.

It was a long and delightful dinner, all the guests giving their compliments freely, Charles taking no praise for himself, giving it all to Bertha and Shirley.

He asked Mr. Miller to tell them all the Christmas story before the band would strike up an evening of music.

So Catherine's father rose to his feet, as resplendent as any of God's saints, and began to speak in his low, modulated voice that carried well throughout the room.

"We're here to celebrate the birth of the Christ Child," he began, and Henry found himself with tears rising in his eyes, unbidden.

"He was, and is to this day, a Gift. He is given to us to turn the fall of Adam into redemption. His life was prophesied for many years, with men searching scripture, trying to pinpoint the time of the Messiah's coming."

He paused for a moment, shifted weight from one foot to the other, gripped the back of his chair.

"When He came, He came in a form of poverty in some wayside stable, not even close to what the people were looking for. And so many did not believe on account of their own preconceived ideas. His message then was humility, as it is now, to humble ourselves to serve Him, accept his life. His death on the cross, His resurrection and saving grace. This evening is held in His honor. For Him, for the indescribable Gift of Life to us who deserve death."

A soft warmth stole over Henry, an awakening of his spirit to recognize that all the suffering, the poverty and the alcoholism, the cruelty of fate, had brought him to see the glory of the Christ child's birth.

Yes, he would seek Him, a youthful, shaking form a few steps behind the wise men, laying down the opulent box containing his whole life, honor, praise, and gratitude.

He squeezed Lila's hand. She looked up, her dark eyes luminous when she saw the tears spill from his eyes.

She knew he had seen the star in the east, was on wings of the spirit to honor Him, and thanked the Lord Jesus with all her heart.

* * *

A cold December moon rose above Juniata Crossing, but inside the stone walls, there was warmth and light and love. The many-paned windows glowed, fireplaces snapped sparks as logs fell, flames grew tall as heat radiated across the room.

In the kitchen, Bertha sat with her great stomach pushing against the folds of her apron, her legs splayed out before her, another cup of wassail at her elbow.

"Well, Shirley, we done pulled it off again. Mark my words, this were one o' the best o' the best. There were a blessing innit. I could feel it in my bones. The Lord told me in my spirit we is honoring Him, the Almighty. Hisself a tiny babe, mind you."

Shirley, who was well on her way to drinking her fourth cup of wassail, looked bleary eyed, but nodded her head in solemn agreement.

"And," Bertha went on, "I'll tell yer another thing. This house has a blessing upon it, with the kindness he gives to every wagon and the beasts drawing it. That there Henry was the beginning of his kindness. Mind you, Shirley, he didn't used to be this way. Meaner than a sharpened axe, when I first got here, mean to him too, and somehow that all changed. There's a blessing, I'm telling you."

* * *

As the violin and fiddle struck up an old Irish reel, the happiness hit Henry and Lila, who joined hands and smiled, swung out on the dance floor, their faces alight with the joy of the season. Charles bowed to Catherine who shook her head, saying softly she had no idea how to dance.

She wasn't fit, this bedraggled, uneducated alcoholic's widow living in a filthy hovel by the side of the river.

She told him that, and his blue eyes with the many lines and folds of skin around them shone into her green ones, quickly filling with tears, and he put a large hand on the small of her back and steered her gently and expertly along.

She hid her face and blinked back the threatening tears, matched her steps to his, felt his muscled power, the magnet of being cared for and guided. She was carried away on the strains of the joyful Christmas music.

The children sat on the sidelines, in awe of their mother, tapping their feet and clapping their hands. Charles grasped little Judith's hands and swung her to the dance floor.

It was a grand Christmas party that night. The snowy hills around the hotel reverberated with music, the moon and stars glittered and twinkled in time to the lyrics.

Charles asked Catherine to stay after all the guests had wended their way up the icy drive. The children had all fallen asleep by the fire, except Belle, who was in the kitchen with Bertha, washing dishes and becoming a bit tipsy on the wassail.

She looked up at him, questioning.

He led her to the adjoining sunroom where a fire crackled and the moon shone through the window-panes on the surrounding snow-covered hills.

He took her hand gently. She drew it away. "What is it, Catherine?"

"I . . . I am not available. Not for you, not anyone."

Shocked, he recoiled.

"But . . ."

"No."

"Catherine, I would be honored if you would hear me out. Listen, I only want to tell you how much I have come to admire you. Your courage and strength, facing insurmountable challenges."

"But I'm old beyond my years. I'm broken in body and spirit. He . . . he . . ."

She bowed her head, shook it from side to side.

"I am not worthy of your love."

The words were spoken in quick staccato, as if saying them fast and hard enough would make him understand, but he reached for her hand, drew her toward himself, very slowly and gently.

"No, don't." She resisted him still.

"Catherine, I love you and want you to be my wife. I would be honored to have these rooms filled with the sound of children's voices, children I have never had."

She shook her head, "I can't. I am only a husk of a woman."

"Then I will take the husk."

Slowly, she lifted her head, courage filling her eyes, and a light beginning to dawn. Like God accepting a sinner, filling him with the works of the Spirit, she must only believe.

He stepped forward and held her gently. She hid her face as she struggled with fear and doubt, her past rising up to mock her, to pull her down in its murky depths.

"Catherine, my offer still stands."

"But my parents."

"The hotel is large. The south side is spacious and well-heated, with no need to go up or down a staircase."

"But we are so many. For so long, we were filthy beggars. Unworthy of this house, these rooms, this home. We are uneducated. Tonight, I had to pretend I knew my manners at the table. We come from nothing."

"I find that hard to believe."

She sighed, words failed her. "May I have some time?"

Her voice wavered, fell.

"I'm afraid I can't let you go. If I do as you wish, you'll tell yourself all these lies and come to believe them."

She swallowed. Her hands fluttered on his sleeves like restless, trapped birds.

"My parents are Anabaptists."

"Catherine, look at me."

She could not.

"This is America, the land of the free. I respect their choice. We are all believers."

Catherine fell against him. Her nervous fingers plucked at his sleeve.

"As am I," she whispered.

"So will you accept my love?" he breathed, barely daring the question.

In answer, she lifted her face, her eyes a portrait of the love she'd hidden away.

* * *

They were married in March. A feast was prepared, and her parents gave their blessing over all.

Still fearful at times, she courageously overcame the doubts to became Mrs. Charles Rusk of the hotel at Juniata Crossing, the grand rooms sounding children's footsteps, laughter, cries when someone was injured, songs and shouting, mud dragged through doors in spring, snow in winter, and dry leaves in fall.

The biggest joy, the unbelievable gift, was an infant born to the two of them when Catherine was forty-three years old and Charles Rusk was older still.

Seasons came and went, the Juniata River rolled on to the Susquehanna, and the hotel built of solid fieldstone presided over the happy family, the parents buried in the graveyard on the north side of Bloody Run, Belle married to the pharmacist's son, living in town like a lady of class.

Henry and Lila stayed in the carriage house for many years, until Henry began breeding and raising Belgian horses and could afford a tract of land adjacent to the hotel where he built a fine house and lived to raise more children in the coming years.

But that one special Christmas season, when Catherine and Henry were gathered back into the arms of Christ, remained a precious diamond in their crown of life.

THE END

About the Author

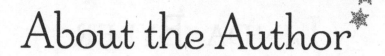

Linda Byler was raised in an Amish family and is an active member of the Amish church today. Growing up, Linda loved to read and write. In fact, she still does. Linda is well known within the Amish community as a columnist for a weekly Amish newspaper. She writes all her novels by hand in notebooks.

Linda is the author of several series of novels, all set among the Amish communities of North America: Lizzie Searches for Love, Sadie's Montana, Lancaster Burning, Hester's Hunt for Home, the Dakota Series, The Long Road Home, New Directions, and the Buggy Spoke Series for younger readers. Linda has also written several Christmas romances set among the Amish: *Mary's Christmas Goodbye, The Christmas Visitor, The Little Amish Matchmaker, Becky Meets Her Match, A Dog for Christmas, A Horse for Elsie, The More the Merrier, A Christmas Engagement,* and *Love Conquers All.* Linda has coauthored *Lizzie's Amish Cookbook: Favorite Recipes from Three Generations of Amish Cooks!, Amish Christmas Cookbook,* and *Amish Soups & Casseroles.*

OTHER BOOKS BY
LINDA BYLER

LIZZIE SEARCHES FOR LOVE SERIES

BOOK ONE   BOOK TWO   BOOK THREE

TRILOGY   COOKBOOK

SADIE'S MONTANA SERIES

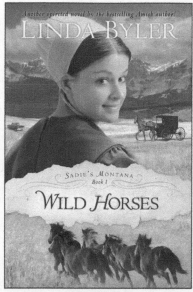

BOOK ONE

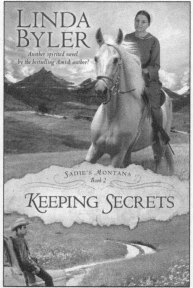

BOOK TWO

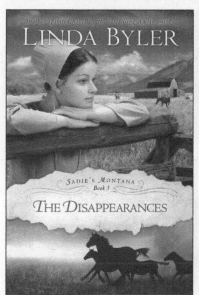

BOOK THREE

TRILOGY

LANCASTER BURNING SERIES

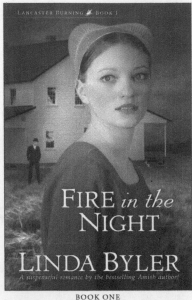

BOOK ONE

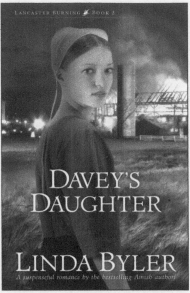

BOOK TWO

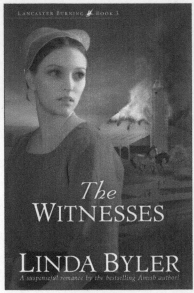

BOOK THREE

TRILOGY

HESTER'S HUNT FOR HOME SERIES

BOOK ONE

BOOK TWO

BOOK THREE

TRILOGY

THE DAKOTA SERIES

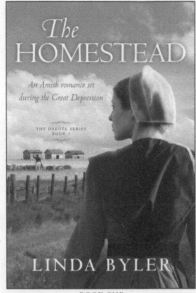

BOOK ONE

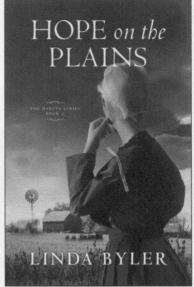

BOOK TWO

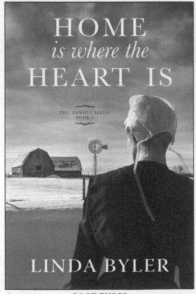

BOOK THREE

TRILOGY

LONG ROAD HOME SERIES

BOOK ONE

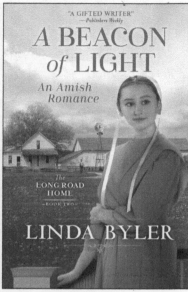

BOOK TWO

BOOK THREE

NEW DIRECTIONS SERIES

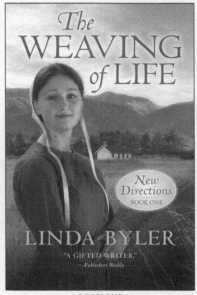

BOOK ONE

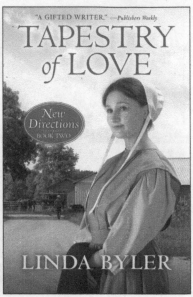

BOOK TWO

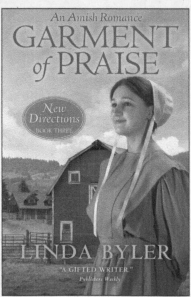

BOOK THREE

STEPPING STONES SERIES

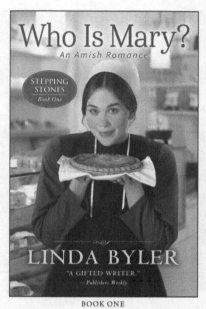

BOOK ONE

COMING SOON

BOOK TWO

COMING SOON

BOOK THREE

CHRISTMAS NOVELLAS

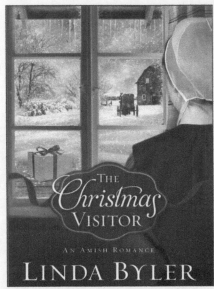

THE CHRISTMAS VISITOR

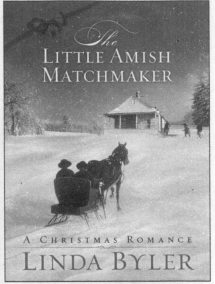

THE LITTLE AMISH MATCHMAKER

MARY'S CHRISTMAS GOODBYE

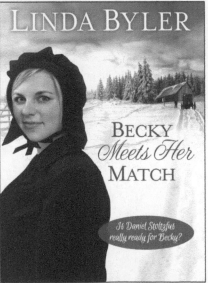

BECKY MEETS HER MATCH

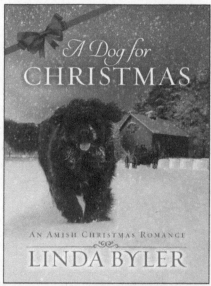

A DOG FOR CHRISTMAS

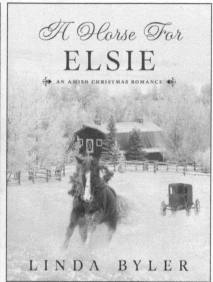

A HORSE FOR ELSIE

THE MORE THE MERRIER

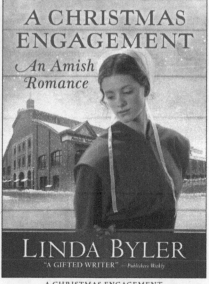

A CHRISTMAS ENGAGEMENT

LOVE CONQUERS ALL

Christmas Collections

AMISH CHRISTMAS ROMANCE COLLECTION

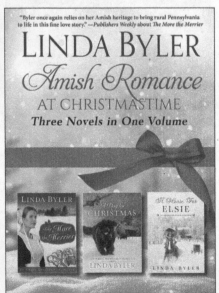

AMISH ROMANCE AT CHRISTMASTIME

STANDALONE NOVELS

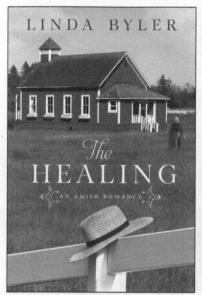

THE HEALING

A SECOND CHANCE

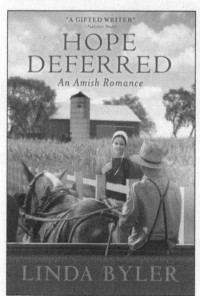

HOPE DEFERRED

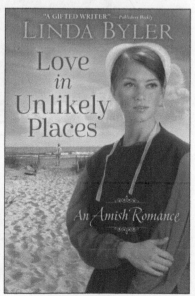

LOVE IN UNLIKELY PLACES

BUGGY SPOKE SERIES FOR YOUNG READERS

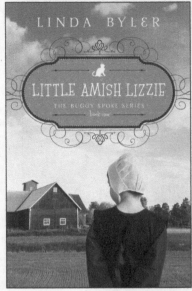

BOOK ONE

BOOK TWO

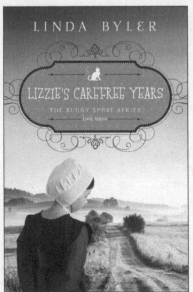

BOOK THREE